A mistake?

"Mike Kalb," Kristin repeated brightly. "He wants me to go to a dinner party."

This has to be a mistake, I thought. *This doesn't make any sense.* "You mean, the Mike who was with us in the car last night?"

Kristin rolled her eyes. "Is it that impossible to believe that he might want to ask me out?"

"I didn't mean that," I said quickly. "Kristin— what—what's the dinner party for?"

Kristin bit her lip. "I'm not sure. Maybe it's some kind of award night? It's a fancy dinner for the whole wrestling team."

I closed my eyes. This conversation was going from bad to worse. He actually did it. Mike actually asked Kristin to the Doggie Chow dinner. Didn't he realize that Billy and I were only kidding about how gross Kristin looked last night? How could Mike do this to a friend of mine?

Don't miss any of the books in SWEET VALLEY JUNIOR HIGH, an exciting new series from Bantam Books!

#1 GET REAL
#2 ONE 2 MANY
#3 SOULMATES
#4 THE COOL CROWD
#5 BOY. FRIEND.

Boy. Friend.

Written by
Jamie Suzanne

Created by
FRANCINE PASCAL

BANTAM BOOKS
NEW YORK · TORONTO · LONDON · SYDNEY · AUCKLAND

RL 4, 008-012

BOY. FRIEND.

A Bantam Book / June 1999

Sweet Valley Junior High is a trademark of
Francine Pascal.

Conceived by Francine Pascal.

Produced by 17th Street Productions,
a division of Daniel Weiss Associates, Inc.
33 West 17th Street, New York, NY 10011.

ISBN: 0-553-48664-0

Published simultaneously in the United States and Canada

Bantam Books are published by Bantam Books, a division of Random
House, Inc. Its trademark, consisting of the words "Bantam Books" and
the portrayal of a rooster, is Registered in the U.S. Patent and Trademark
Office and in other countries. Marca Registrada. Bantam Books, 1540
Broadway, New York, New York 10036.

PRINTED IN THE UNITED STATES OF AMERICA

OPM   0 9 8 7 6 5 4 3 2 1

To Jamie Stewart

Kristin

"Kristin! Watch out!"

I whirled around to see what Brian was talking about. Too late. An ocean of sticky pink punch showered down onto my head. My hair was completely soaked.

"Uh. I guess I shouldn't have put the bowl on top of the refrigerator, huh?" Brian asked in a sheepish voice.

I just stood there with my eyes closed for a moment, counting to ten. *Why did I even volunteer to help Jessica Wakefield clean up in the first place?* I thought. Actually, I knew the answer to that. I liked Jessica. I had to respect the way she wasn't afraid to stand up to people who treated her wrong. She stood up to my best friend, Lacey Frells, once—and I know that's not easy. And tonight Jessica had tossed a bunch of drunk high-school guys out of her party— which had been the biggest bash of the year until it got a little out of control. Okay, majorly out of control. Now Jessica was trying to put the living room back together while here I was, standing in her kitchen, covered in sticky goo.

I rolled my eyes. "Oh, Brian," was all I could say.

He handed me a paper towel, and I tried to blot my hair dry. That's when Brian burst out laughing. "It's not funny," I insisted. Then I looked down at my sweater. I had already spilled punch on it earlier in the evening, and I was now definitely getting the multilayered tie-dyed effect. I giggled. I might look horrible, but at least I could claim I was retro. "Okay," I admitted, "it is pretty funny."

Brian laughed even harder. "You look great as a redhead," he said. "I mean, as a pink head. That color makes your eyes look really blue."

I gave him a lopsided smile, wondering whether he actually meant that. I didn't really care—it was a nice thing for him to say whether he meant it or not. It's pretty hard to get mad at Brian, even when he acts like a total space case. Hard, but not impossible.

"When did this night go so wrong?" I asked no one in particular.

Brian considered a moment. "I think about the time the cops showed up."

We both cracked up. No doubt about it . . . this had been one wild party.

But that's another story.

I looked back down at my soaked clothes and made another attempt to dry them with the paper towel. "Great," I said as bits of paper towel came off all over my outfit. "This new sweater is toast," I moaned. "My mother's going to kill me—we just bought it!"

"Maybe she'll think you've improved it. That sweater wasn't really your color anyway."

I finally gave up scrubbing at my sweater and glared at Brian. Couldn't he stop joking for one minute? "Like I really want fashion advice from someone who obviously doesn't even know his own pants size."

Brian looked hurt. "What's that supposed to mean?"

Instead of his usual tidy khakis and T-shirt, Brian was wearing baggy jeans, an even baggier green sweatshirt, and, to top it off, a hideous, faded brown baseball cap. He had pulled the cap backward over his longish blond hair so that it totally covered his eyebrows.

Brian glanced down at his outfit. "My sister said this look was way cool," he told me.

"Well, Addie thinks Ronald McDonald dresses cool," I said. "And that's exactly who you look like. Why don't you get some big, floppy shoes to go with the rest of your enormous clothes?"

We just stood there a minute, staring at each other. I think he was pretty surprised that I'd just gone off like that. Usually I keep my cool. But it was late, and I was tired. I guess that was why I didn't feel like apologizing right then.

"I'd better find Jessica," I said finally, heading through the door. "Maybe she'll lend me a dry shirt to change into."

"I'll call and get us a ride home," Brian said. "And don't worry—wet or dry, you'll always be beautiful to me!" I heard him chuckle.

If only. I sighed. I've had a crush on Brian since the sixth grade. Of course, I'd never tell him that. We're really good friends, and I don't want things to get weird just because I think Brian is cuter than Hanson and twice as nice.

Jessica nearly dropped the broom she was using to sweep the living room when she saw me. "What happened to you?"

"Don't ask," I told her.

Bethel McCoy was crouched on the floor, sweeping paper into a dustpan. "You're a mess," she said. Bethel is never one to mince words.

I nodded. "Tell me about it. So, Jessica, could I borrow a shirt or something?"

"Sure," she said. "Elizabeth's upstairs. She'll show you where the bathroom is and where my T-shirts are. Take whatever you need."

"Thanks," I said, heading for the stairs.

I found Jessica's twin cleaning up in her room. She gaped at me. "What happened to you?"

"I got into a fight," I explained. "The punch bowl won. Jessica said I could borrow a T-shirt."

Elizabeth waved me into the bathroom. "Why don't you clean up first?" she suggested. "I'll find you something to wear."

I tried to get clean, but my hair was a total disaster. One big, gooey strand hung over my forehead, plastered down with sticky punch. I tucked the rest of my hair behind my ears, but that one strand kept falling out.

Then I washed my face. Unfortunately, my formerly carefully applied mascara created a raccoon effect under my eyes. The only difference being that raccoons are cute.

I studied myself in the mirror. Pulling my hair behind my ears made my face look totally round. We are talking Night of the Living Doughnut. Usually I think I look pretty good. Don't get me wrong—supermodels don't have to worry about the competition or anything, but Lacey always tell me that I have pretty eyes and nice hair. And she's not the kind who would lie.

Pretty eyes weren't going to save me now, though. The sweater that formerly fell nicely at my waist was now stuck to my stomach in an extremely unflattering way. I sighed. *Maybe my mom is right,* I thought. *Maybe I should just lose a few pounds.*

I frowned, remembering all of the diets she'd tried to put me on. There was one all-grapefruit number that was supposed to be "very cleansing." I actually did lose weight on that diet—mostly because grapefruit makes me want to barf. But usually I never lost more than a couple of pounds, and I could never keep it off. I've tried to explain to my mom that we just have different bodies—that I wasn't made to be skinny like her—but she always says that I could be a model too if I had more "willpower." I mean, give me a break. My mom eats like a pig and never gains a pound. I eat healthy food and am considered overweight. But who cares? I'm sure not going to start eating unhealthy stuff just so I can be fifteen pounds lighter. It's not like that's going to solve all of my problems or something.

Besides, I don't usually look like Night of the Living Doughnut. I would just try to keep from drowning in a bowl of punch from now on.

"Kristin!" Brian yelled from downstairs. "Our ride's here!"

"Here's a shirt," Elizabeth said as I flung open the bathroom door.

"Thanks," I replied, "but I think I should just

get going. I borrowed your hair clip, by the way."

"No problem," Elizabeth reassured me with a smile. "Thanks for helping us clean up. See you Monday."

"See you," I said, and hurried down the stairs. "Bye, Jessica!" I called. "Bye, Bethel!"

"Bye," they chorused as I walked out the door.

I was so happy to be going home that I grinned to myself all the way down the front walk. But the minute I scrambled into the car beside Brian, I thought I might die. Brian's brother, Billy, was behind the wheel. That wasn't the part that made me want to die, even though Billy is sixteen and a sophomore at Sweet Valley High.

No, the problem was that Billy had brought a friend along. And not just any friend—Mike Kalb! Mike is sixteen and completely gorgeous. We are talking black-haired, green-eyed, total all that-ness. I nearly crawled under the floor mat when he turned around.

"Hey, Brian, how's it going?" Mike asked, then nodded at me politely. "Hey," he said.

I swallowed. "Hey, yourself," I said, nearly in a whisper. *So he didn't recognize me,* I thought, actually relieved. Mike is good friends with Lacey's boyfriend, Gel. I didn't want him to think I normally went to parties looking like this.

At that very moment Billy turned around in

the front seat. "Brian, you didn't tell me this was a swimming party," he said.

"It wasn't," Brian told him.

"Then how come Kristin looks like a drowned rat?" Mike laughed at his own joke. Sometimes he seems to think he's my older brother too.

"That's so funny and original," I said sarcastically. I would have added a snappy comeback, but I was too tired. Besides, I figured I could let one lame joke slide.

I turned to say something to Brian, which is when I noticed that Mike was looking at me with a weird expression on his face. Like he was studying me. My eyes met his, and for a split second I felt a tiny burst of excitement.

Is he interested in me? I wondered. *He couldn't be—could he? Not tonight. I look like a total loser!*

I blinked and looked down just as Billy started yammering on about some stupid wrestling match. I knew he and Mike were both on the SVH team.

Billy pulled up to my house. He and Mike were so busy talking that they barely noticed when I jumped out. "Thanks for the ride," I said anyway. Brian gave me a big smile.

"Take care, rat girl," he joked. But he didn't make a move to get out of the car and walk me to my door.

I tried not to feel disappointed.

I opened my mouth to say good-bye to Brian, but Billy raced the engine. Showing off as usual. The car sped away.

Forget it, I told myself. *You and Brian are friends. And that's all you'll ever be.*

Brian

"I am totally wiped," I announced to Billy and Mike. "Just get me home quick so I can collapse into bed."

I slumped down on the backseat and tried to stretch my legs, which is pretty hard, considering how small the back of our car is. With five kids in the family, you'd think my dad would spring for a minivan or something. But he says this little car is cheaper.

"Sleep!" Billy sounded shocked. "Are you kidding? The night is young."

"Don't think we're letting you go," Mike added. He leered at me over the back of the seat, curling his hands into monsterlike claws. "Vat you vant is blood," he said in a vampire voice. "Lots of blood."

"Don't tell me you want to go to the movies," I said. "It's already past eleven o'clock!"

"Vat?" Mike pretended to be horrified. "Ve missed one show already!"

"Relax." Billy chuckled. "The horror fest runs all night long. Dad already said you could come with us, Brian."

"No way," I said. "Drop me off. I'm too tired."

"Whoa—you're too tired? Who are you, my grandma?" Mike asked.

"Quit being so pathetic, Brian," Billy said. "This is going to be a blast!"

"It's just that I—," I began.

"Seriously, man, you should be thanking us," Mike interrupted. "I mean, how often do we ask you to hang with us—all night?"

Billy shook his head. Then he sighed. "I don't know, baby bro," he said. "I thought you were growing up. . . ."

I rolled my eyes. Billy lives to give me a hard time. I knew he'd never take no for an answer.

I looked at Billy's grinning face in the rearview mirror. "Come on, it'll be fun," he prodded. "It's just one little all-night monster fest," he added.

I laughed. "All right, all right. I know I'll be sorry tomorrow. But you guys can talk anybody into anything."

"Yeah?" Mike grinned. "Hey, Billy, why don't you loan me a hundred bucks? Or maybe you could be my driver for my big date next weekend?"

"What big date?" I asked.

"The Doggie Chow dinner," Billy replied.

Mike punched Billy on the arm. "That's a secret, butt-head!"

"Ouch!" Billy glared at Mike. "Dude, you must develop the will to chill. Brian's cool."

"Yeah, I'm cool," I said. "So tell me all about it."

Mike turned to look at me and stuck his finger in my face. "You have to swear you won't tell anyone."

"I won't," I promised. Why were they acting like such freaks? Who was Mike's date anyway— Jennifer Love Hewitt?

"Okay." Mike settled back into his seat. "You know how the wrestling team has a secret club?"

"Of course he knows," Billy answered for me. "I told him about it. He's going to pledge when he gets to high school."

"You mean the Secret Order of Golden Moose?" I sat up, interested now. Wrestling wasn't really my sport, but I was psyched to join the team in high school, all right. Billy had been a member of the team and the order for a year now, and all of the cool guys at Sweet Valley High were in it too. All my brother's friends. I knew I would dig hanging with them. Of course, if Coach Robinson ever found out about the secret club, it would be history. I just hoped that wouldn't happen until long after I'd graduated from Sweet Valley High.

"Right. Every year there's a different initiation rite for new pledges," Mike explained. "This year is the best. The Doggie Chow is a big, fancy dinner party. The joke is, the guys bring the ugliest girl they can find. Real dogs. Then we serve doggie chow for dinner."

Was I missing something? That didn't sound very funny to me. "That's supposed to be a joke?" I asked Mike. "You're really going to do that to some girl?"

"Sure. Why not?" Mike replied. "I want to pledge."

"You have to pledge," Billy told him. "I've been dying for you to join."

"Hold on," I said, turning to Billy. "You didn't go to your own initiation last year, remember?"

"I was sick, Brian," Billy said in a warning voice. That's when I remembered: Billy hadn't wanted to go to his initiation because he said it was stupid, so he pretended to be sick and stayed home. I thought it was cool that he hadn't done his dumb initiation pledge, but the secret order got really mad and almost didn't let him into the club. Luckily Billy had a couple of really good friends who pulled for him. "Besides," Billy went on, "the order has changed the rules since then. Now if you skip, you're out."

"So there's no way I'm bagging. Anyway," Mike added, "so what if it's dumb? Getting through one dinner isn't a big deal."

13

"Maybe not for you," I said. "But I bet your date will think differently. Who are you taking?" I couldn't think of anyone I would ever take to a party like that, no matter how much I wanted to get into a club.

"I don't know yet," Mike admitted. "I kind of don't want to ask anyone I might ever see again."

"You'd better find someone quick," Billy told him. "Girls like plenty of notice for a dinner date."

"Yeah, yeah. I'll think of something," Mike replied.

"I don't know, Mike," I said. "Can't you think of any way to get out of this? It sounds really mean."

"The club is worth it. You'll see when you join, Brian." Billy's voice said "subject closed," so I didn't say anything else. Well—what did I know about it? I wasn't even in the club . . . yet. Besides, Billy doesn't do mean things. If he thought this dinner was okay, then it was. He caught me looking at him in the rearview mirror and grinned again. "The fabulous Rainey brothers will rule together!"

"With me," Mike reminded him.

We pulled into the Cinema Six parking lot. A small bunch of kids were hanging out in front of the main doors. *Good,* I thought. At least there wasn't a huge, long line. I hated waiting on line. And waiting for something I didn't want to see in the first place was the absolute worst.

Billy parked up front, and we crossed the lot and entered the lobby. Billy and Mike nodded to some of their friends, high-school kids I didn't know.

"I've got it!" Billy suddenly exclaimed as we reached the ticket window. "I know who your date should be."

"Who?" Mike asked.

"It's someone you saw tonight," Billy told Mike.

Mike looked puzzled, so Billy gave him a hint. "Think about someone with a pink-goo hairdo."

"Kristin?" I spun around and stared at Billy in shock.

He shrugged. "Why not? She'd be perfect." He grinned.

I glared at him. "Forget it," I snapped. "No way. Kristin's a friend of mine. Besides," I added, "she's not usually covered in punch. She's usually pretty."

"Pretty awful," Mike cracked. "Especially that stringy piece of hair that kept falling down between her eyes."

Billy hooted. I snorted a laugh too. I couldn't help it. That strand of hair really was gross.

"Oh, Kristin," Billy cooed, "your hair is like a beautiful . . . Easter egg!" He winked at me.

"Come on, Billy, cut it out," I pleaded.

"Ease up, Brian," Billy said, his eyes twinkling. "I'm just kidding. And you have to admit, Kristin looked pretty hilarious."

15

I grinned, picturing her.

Billy took the opportunity to start teasing again. "Could you imagine Mike out on a date with her? Kristin, my darling, please let me run my fingers through your hair. . . ."

I couldn't help chuckling—the image was just too funny.

"Ohmigosh! I'm stuck to your head!" Billy went on. He put his hand on Mike's head and pretended he couldn't pry it off.

Mike and I practically doubled over, we were laughing so hard. Their high-school friends were staring, of course. But I guess they're used to Billy clowning around.

"Darling Kristin, now we'll be together forever." Billy put his other hand over his heart and batted his eyelashes.

My brother is such a goofball, I thought. *I can't believe I actually thought he was serious about Mike asking Kristin to the Doggie Chow.*

I was still laughing when we all piled into the theater and grabbed the best seats, not too far up front and smack in the center of the row.

It was great hanging with Billy and Mike— and it would get even better once we were all in high school.

The fabulous Raineys rule, I thought. *With Mike.*

A n n a

Dear Diary,

I can't believe I did that. I can't believe I ran out of Elizabeth's party last night like a big freak. It's just that whenever I see people drinking, I remember Tim and that horrible night. . . .

Sometimes I forget it's even happened. I'll get all caught up in my everyday life and I'll feel like a normal person instead of like Anna, The Girl Whose Brother Was Killed by a Drunk Driver.

But it never lasts.

I was so grateful Salvador came after me last night. Of course he knew where I was. The porch swing, where else?

Sometimes I wonder what I would do without Salvador. Go crazy, I guess. Who else would just let me cry and cry until I'm so exhausted that I'm practically falling asleep?

Nobody. Except maybe Elizabeth.

I can't believe I thought she had yanked the

Anna

poem I wrote for Tim from the 'zine. When Salvador told me she just moved it to another page, I felt like an idiot. I should have known Elizabeth would never do something like that without telling me about it. I mean, she has the right to play around with the layout if she wants, right? If she thinks the poem would look better on page two than on page one, maybe I should listen to her. After all, she's the only one of us who knows what she's doing.

And I know she wouldn't hurt my feelings on purpose.

I didn't see much of her at the party. I wonder where she was all night?

Salvador

Dear Diary,

Yes!

I kissed Elizabeth last night!

All right!

I am The Man!

So what do I do now?

I don't really know what Elizabeth thinks about it. I hope she's as psyched as I am. But if she were psyched, wouldn't she have called me this morning?

Maybe my kiss was really slimy and she's totally grossed out right now. Or maybe she's telling Jessica all about it and laughing her head off. Oh, man. I hope that isn't happening.

What should I do? Normally I would ask Anna's advice, but she's got real problems. I can't even imagine telling her about this right now.

I guess I'll just wait for a sign from Elizabeth.

Kristin

I stared at my clock for about the thousandth time. 10:26. This morning was crawling by. I grabbed my brush and forced myself to run it through my hair one hundred strokes just to kill time.

10:28.

Come on, move! I silently ordered.

10:29.

Only one minute to go.

I'd promised myself I would not call Lacey one minute before ten-thirty. Lacey absolutely hates to get up early on Sunday morning. Actually, she totally forbade me ever to call before eleven, but this couldn't wait. This news was big. And I mean major.

Click.

10:30.

Finally! I leaped for the phone and punched in Lacey's number. Ring, ring, ring . . . What if she didn't answer?

Her answering machine clicked on. I waited for the tone to record. "Lacey! It's me," I nearly shouted. "Listen, I know it's too early to call. But you absolutely have to call me back the instant you get up because something really, really big just hap—"

"Hello?" Lacey's voice interrupted. "Kristin?" She yawned into the phone. "Okay, what's the big deal? And it had better be important because—"

"Oh, it's important, all right," I told her. I took a breath to steady my voice. It was actually shaking with excitement.

"I just had a phone call," I began. "Asking me for a date on Friday!"

"Who?" Lacey sounded vaguely interested now. "Mike Kalb!"

There was a moment of silence. "Mike Kalb?" she repeated. "*The* Mike Kalb? Mike Gorgeous Kalb? No way!"

"I know." I grinned into the phone, even though Lacey couldn't see me. "And Lacey—get this—it's for a fancy dinner. It's some kind of wrestling-team thing at Jordan Kander's house. Mike made it sound like a pretty big deal. And I'm going to meet all of his friends!"

"Oh, Kristin, this is big," Lacey said in a solemn voice. "This is huge! But wait. Back up.

How did this happen?" she asked. "I didn't even know you guys knew each other."

"We don't, not really." I explained about my ride home from the Wakefield twins' party and how Mike seemed interested in me even though I was a total mess. And then on the phone this morning he was so nice. He said he could tell we had a lot in common and that I was easy to talk to and stuff like that.

"That just shows he has great taste," Lacey declared. "He can already see how terrific you are. Besides, I'm sure you didn't look half as bad as you think."

I felt a surge of pleasure. It really was great to be picked out by a cool guy like Mike.

"This is so fantastic!" Lacey went on. "We can double-date and everything!"

"I know, I thought of that too," I said. "Double dating would be so much fun."

An image of the four of us cruising around in Gel's car flashed through my head, making me smile again. I would never have said anything to Lacey, but I always envied her for having a boyfriend. Especially an older guy like Gel. She always got to go to cool parties without me since I didn't like going places where I didn't know anyone. I always felt kind of like a baby when she told me about the cool stuff she'd done over the weekend.

But now we could hang out all the time!

If Mike and I hit it off, that is.

"I cannot believe this," Lacey said. "Your whole life has changed overnight."

"Well, it might change," I corrected her. "If the date goes okay."

"If? If!" Lacey shrieked. "Forget 'if.' This has got to be the best date ever, Kristin. Absolutely nothing can go wrong. It's just way too important. Now let's figure out what you should wear."

Lacey started talking about outfits, but I zoned out. Suddenly I had major butterflies. Could I really pull off the perfect date? I'd barely been on a date before, much less with an older guy.

"Lacey," I interrupted. "Wait. I don't know how to act on a date with someone like Mike. What will we talk about? What if I freeze and can't say anything? What if—"

"Calm down," Lacey told me. "First dates are no big deal. Look—Mike already likes you, right? Plus we have almost a whole week to get ready. I'll come over, and we'll make plans right away. But first I'll call Gel and find out everything I can about Mike."

"No!" I shouted. "Don't you dare ask Gel to help! I'd be so embarrassed."

"Take it easy," Lacey told me. "I won't do it in

an obvious way. Besides, I already know lots of stuff about Mike."

"Like what?" I asked.

"Like he's really into scuba diving," Lacey began.

"Scuba diving?" I blurted out. "Are we supposed to talk about that? As if I know the first thing about it!"

"How do you feel about dirt-bike racing?" Lacey asked.

"Ugh. It's dumb, and it scares me," I admitted.

Lacey laughed. "No one said you had to do this stuff with Mike," she pointed out. "All you have to do is talk about it. You just have to know enough to keep a conversation going."

I felt a lot better when she said that. My call waiting beeped. "Hold on, Lacey," I told her.

I clicked over to the other line. It was Brian, reminding me that we had plans to meet at Vito's today.

"Lacey," I said. "That was Brian. I forgot I promised to meet him for pizza later."

"Who cares? This date is more important than a pizza with Brian," Lacey said. "Just blow him off."

I rolled my eyes. Typical Lacey advice. "I can't," I told her. "I wouldn't feel right about it. Friends are important too, you know."

"As important as your first big date?" Lacey demanded.

I hesitated. "I know, why don't you meet us at Vito's? We could talk then."

"Okay," Lacey agreed. "But don't make plans with Brian for this evening. We have a lot of work to do."

Elizabeth

Dear Diary,

Isn't this sick? I'm actually happy to be grounded.

By the time Mom and Dad got home from their trip to Vancouver this afternoon, we had cleaned the place up really well. But then our next-door neighbor called Dad and told him that we'd had a party and that the cops had been here.

Dad got really mad, which is something that I've only seen maybe once before in my life, and he said that if we couldn't be trusted to make our own rules, then he and Mom would make the rules for us. (Or something like that.) The upshot was, after a one-hour lecture by our parents about how disappointed in us they were, Steven, Jessica, and I were heavily grounded. No TV, no phone, no leaving the house for any reason except school for two weeks.

So why am I happy? Because I don't have to

26

talk to Salvador about the fact that we kissed or to Anna about the fact that she never told me her brother was killed by a drunk driver. Salvador is so cute, and Anna is such a good friend—but I'm confused. What should I say to them? But now it doesn't make any difference because I can't talk to them. At school I never see them alone, and at home I'm not allowed to talk to anyone except for members of my family.

It'll give me some time to think—to figure things out.

Besides, if I want someone to talk to, there's always Jessica.

Brian

"Brian!" Kristin waved me over to a booth.

"Hey," I said, sliding into the seat across from her. "How did you manage to beat me here?"

"I don't know." Kristin lifted her eyebrows. "But you look like you're dragging a bit."

"True," I admitted. "Billy forced me to go out after we dropped you off. Monster fest," I explained.

Kristin shook her head. "Figures." Then she smiled. She has the greatest smile—it changes her whole face. She leaned toward me. "Guess what," she said in a whisper.

I dropped my voice and leaned forward too. "What?" It isn't like Kristin to act all *Mission Impossible,* so I figured whatever she had to say must be important.

"Somebody asked me out on a date this morning."

I stared at her a minute, unsure what to say.

Suddenly I had this weird feeling, like I was watching this scene from outside of my body. Like it was happening to somebody else.

"Well?" she asked.

What was she expecting? Like—congratulations or something? I felt weird saying that, so instead I asked, "Who was it?"

She got all dreamy eyed. "Mike Kalb."

I went cold. "What?" I asked quietly.

"Mike Kalb," she repeated brightly. "He wants me to go to a dinner party."

This has to be a mistake, I thought. *This doesn't make any sense.* "You mean, the Mike who was with us in the car last night?"

Kristin rolled her eyes. "Is it that impossible to believe that he might want to ask me out?"

"I didn't mean that," I said quickly. "Kristin— what—what's the dinner party for?"

Kristin bit her lip. "I'm not sure. Maybe it's some kind of award night? It's a fancy dinner for the whole wrestling team."

I closed my eyes. This conversation was going from bad to worse. He actually did it. Mike actually asked Kristin to the Doggie Chow dinner. Didn't he realize that Billy and I were only kidding about how gross Kristin looked last night? How could Mike do this to a friend of mine?

How could he do it to me?

I opened my eyes again to see Kristin staring at me, a concerned expression on her face. "Are you okay?" she asked.

"Fine," I said, but it came out all squeaky. I hate that. I looked into her blue eyes, feeling a wave of indignation. Kristin wasn't ugly. Not a bit. Actually, I thought she was one of the prettiest girls in school. Definitely the prettiest in our class. I couldn't believe Mike thought Kristin was a dog! Besides, she's really nice and doesn't deserve to be treated like dirt. Not that anybody does.

"What did he say to you?" I asked, trying to keep the anger out of my voice. "What did you say to him?"

Kristin grinned. "You're totally shocked." She opened her eyes wide. "I know—when Mike called, I was pretty surprised too. It's not like we ever hung out together. We never even talked much before. And suddenly there he was, asking me out!" She giggled, which actually made me feel nauseated. "Even after I looked so awful last night."

"You didn't look that bad," I protested.

"Whatever, Brian," she replied. "Obviously that kind of stuff doesn't matter to Mike. Still," she went on, "I plan to look a lot better at this dinner. Now I just have to decide what to wear. Lacey thinks I should go strapless. Nothing low cut, you know. Just very dressy." Kristin leaned back against the booth. "To tell you the truth, I'm kind of nervous," she said. "Lacey says I have to be the perfect date, like in some magazine article. Make his interests my interests, that kind of stuff. And now I'm feeling a little paranoid about the whole thing."

"Yeah," I said absently. Kristin had no idea that the whole date was a mean prank. She thought it was a big deal—her biggest night ever. How could I tell her the truth? How could I say, "Actually, Kristin, it doesn't matter what you wear since Mike will want you to look as horrendous as possible"? Answer: I couldn't.

Kristin looked even more thoughtful. "I don't know. Maybe the magazines are right. It makes sense to have something to talk about with a date," she told me. "Especially on a first date. I'd hate to sit there like an idiot, with nothing to say to him all night."

I just sat there. I pictured Kristin at the dinner, in a new dress, thrilled to be with Mike. I imagined the moment when she found out the truth . . . when she realized it had all been a horrible joke. . . . I imagined her face then. . . .

"Oh no!" Kristin sat up with a horrified look on her face. "I have to know about wrestling! Brian, you have to help me! I know nothing about the high-school team. Have they won

most of their matches this year or lost or what?"
She looked totally panic-stricken.

"Yeah. Sure. Wrestling." I swallowed. This was
awful. This was terrible.

I had to warn her. I couldn't let her go
through with this date. What about when she
realized she was supposed to be a dog? A loser? I
knew Kristin worried about her weight. She'd
freak out.

And it was my fault because of that stupid
punch bowl, I realized. If I hadn't set the dumb
bowl on the refrigerator, it wouldn't have spilled
all over her and she would've looked pretty. Not
like a drowned rat.

And Mike never would have asked her on this
loser date. I could kick myself!

"I'm starting to worry about you," Kristin
said, peering at me. "You have the weirdest look
on your face."

"Do I?" I bluffed. "I mean, it's just that, well,
you know, you never went out with a guy like
Mike Kalb before. Maybe you shouldn't rush
into this thing."

She looked bewildered. "Brian, I'm not mar-
rying the guy."

"B-But that's my point," I stammered. I had to
stop this date, but I didn't know what to say that
would make Kristin not want to go. "It's your

first date with him, and, uh, well, you've never even gone on a date with a guy in high school before." I knew I sounded like a moron, but I just couldn't think of anything better. "Are you sure you can handle this?"

"There's a first time for everything, right?" Kristin was starting to look annoyed.

"Sure," I said. "But I don't know. Maybe it's better to ease into something like this. Get to know some other high-school guys first. Right! Like, talk to one or two other guys on the phone first. And then decide if you want to date a guy like Mike."

"Brian, you're babbling."

I heaved an exasperated sigh and ran my fingers through my hair. What now? *She isn't buying this. She's going to go on this date and be humiliated, and it will be all my fault. . . .* "I just think that this is a mistake—," I started.

Kristin crossed her arms over her chest and glared. "What are you saying, Brian?"

"Nothing," I told her. "Just what I said, that's all."

"You think Mike made a mistake?" she demanded. "You think he shouldn't go out with someone like me?"

"No. I was just agreeing with you," I answered. I was trying really hard to say things the right way so it would come out like friendly advice and not like the harsh truth. "You're the one who said this was all a big surprise," I reminded her. "Maybe you're right. Maybe you should break this date and start with something smaller. You know."

"You don't think I'm cool enough to date Mike." Kristin's voice was flat and angry. She shot me a dirty look. Then her eyes filled up with tears.

Please, please, don't cry, I silently willed. I couldn't stand it when girls cried. When one of my little sisters cried, I always got this terrible helpless feeling.

"I can't believe this," Kristin went on. Her voice got all small and choked up. "A cool guy wants to go out with me, and you can't even imagine how that might be possible. Thanks a lot, Brian. That really makes me feel great."

"I'm sorry," I told her. "It's just that . . . I only meant . . ." I paused.

"I know what you meant," Kristin said bitterly. "You made it perfectly clear."

"Kristin, c'mon. You're twisting my words around." I tried to smile, as if I could kid her out of it. I didn't know what else to do.

Billy, I thought. *Billy is great with girls. He never gets flustered by tears. I'll call Billy and ask his advice,* I decided. Besides, this whole thing was his fault just as much as it was mine. Why did he have to be such a comedian all the time?

"Uh, listen, I forgot—I have to call home," I told Kristin, leaping to my feet. "Wait right here. I'll be back in a second."

"You're leaving?" Kristin's mouth fell open. "Now?"

"I have to," I said. There are just some things I can't handle on my own.

I raced to the pay phone and punched in my number. Thankfully, Billy answered the phone. "Billy, you've got to help me. Mike actually asked Kristin to the dog dinner, and she thinks it's a big date, and I don't know what to do!"

Billy sucked in his breath. "I can't believe he did that," he said. "Didn't he realize we were joking?"

"I don't know! So—should I tell Kristin the truth or have Mike cancel or what?"

There was a pause. "Look, Brian," Billy said finally. "You can't tell Kristin about the dinner. It would ruin things for Mike. He has to get into the order."

What? I stared at the phone. Had everyone gone insane overnight? "Mike could find another date," I suggested quickly. "That way Kristin won't get hurt, and Mike will still be initiated."

"I don't know," Billy began. "It's kind of late notice already."

"It's almost a week away!" I cried.

"Yeah, but it isn't easy to find another girl. . . ."

"You have to get him to find someone else," I

begged Billy. If anyone could take care of this situation, my brother could. I knew Billy wouldn't let Kristin get hurt. "Mike won't listen to me, but he'll listen to you, Billy. Please! Do it for me."

Billy paused. "Okay, I'll try," he promised.

I felt tons better. "Thanks, Billy," I said.

"No problem, little bro."

I hung up and took a deep breath. Okay, that was taken care of. Kristin didn't know it, but she owed me—big.

Kristin

I think I was still sitting there, shocked, when the door to Vito's burst open. Lacey strode in, followed by three girls I didn't know. She spotted me right away and waved.

I waved back. I tried to smile, but I was still stewing about Brian. I couldn't believe the way he turned against me. And then just left me sitting there!

I checked my watch again. He'd been gone a good eight minutes. And that's a long time when you're sitting alone in a place like Vito's.

"Hi!" Lacey said as she dropped onto the end of my booth. I scooted over to make room for her. "I hope you don't mind, but I couldn't wait for you to meet my high-school friends. They aren't staying anyway." She pointed to the three girls, who were placing orders up at the to-go counter. "Annie, Janine, and Tara," she said, naming each one. "I know them through Gel. Tara goes to private school, but Annie and

Janine are at Sweet Valley High," she added.

"Oh. Really," I said.

Lacey squinted at me. "Yes, and I thought you'd be glad to know them. For when you start dating Mike and all."

"If I do," I said.

Lacey looked astonished. "What do you mean, 'if'?"

I tried to explain what just happened with Brian. I mean, maybe Brian had a point. Maybe I couldn't pull off this date with Mike.

"I don't believe this," Lacey fumed. "Brian is such a jerk. I'm so glad you're going out with Mike so you can finally get over your dumb crush on Brian. You've always been way too cool for him. Believe me, Brian doesn't know what he's talking about. And I'm going to tell him so the minute he comes back."

"You really think so?" I asked, relieved. "You don't think I'm making a mistake?"

Lacey groaned. "Your only mistake was listening to Brian. He is such an idiot."

"Don't say that, Lacey. Brian always means well. I just wish I knew why he said those things."

Lacey shrugged. "Who knows? Did you do something to hurt his feelings?" she asked.

"I'm not sure," I admitted. Had I done anything? I thought back to the party last night.

"The only thing . . . no, it's too stupid to count," I said.

Lacey cocked an eyebrow. "Nothing's too stupid when it comes to boys," she declared. "Spill."

I shrugged. "I teased him about his clothes last night," I told her. "He had on this really baggy outfit and a backward baseball cap, remember? Like he thought he was Puff Daddy. So I teased him."

"I remember. He deserved to be mocked," Lacey cracked.

"Actually, I thought he looked adorable," I admitted. "But maybe he was insulted. Maybe he's sensitive about his appearance."

Lacey raised her eyebrows. "Brian? Sensitive? Are we talking about Brian Rainey?"

I thought about it. Brian was so easygoing. Nobody could insult him, especially about something as dumb as clothes.

"Believe me, he's oblivious to stuff like that. In fact, he's pretty oblivious, period." Lacey shook her head. "Which is why it's so perfect that Mike came along to save you from wasting yourself on Brian. So quit worrying about him."

"I can't help it," I defended myself. "We've been friends forever, and—"

I stopped talking as Annie, Janine, and Tara came

over. Tara balanced a pizza box, and the others carried cold drinks. Tara set the box on the table.

"We can only stay a few minutes," Tara said, shaking her light brown bob out of her face. "But we'll have a drink with you guys."

"This is Kristin," Lacey said.

I smiled at the three girls. "Hi."

"Nice to meet you," Tara said, and the other girls said hello. Annie had long red hair, and Janine had a fountain of brown curls falling from a ponytail on top of her head. We slid farther over in the booth to make room for Tara. Annie and Janine sat across from us.

"We should leave a place for Brian," I told them.

"Brian Rainey," Lacey explained. "Billy Rainey's little brother."

"Billy's brother?" Annie's green eyes grew wide. "Hey—are you the Kristin they were talking about last night at the movies?"

"Probably," I admitted. "Why—what were they saying?"

"Nothing," Tara said quickly. She gave Annie a meaningful glance.

Whatever the meaning was, Annie didn't get it. "Tara, don't you remember?" she asked. "Billy and his brother were totally dissing some girl named Kristin."

What? I stared at Tara, who was glaring at Annie.

"Are you kidding?" I asked weakly.

"No," Janine said. "But he couldn't have been talking about you. The Kristin he was talking about had gross hair."

"And you don't," Tara assured me. "You have really pretty hair, so it must have been a different person."

"Oh yeah," I said, nodding. What else could I say? Of course, I knew Brian had been talking about me. I felt like I'd just been stabbed in the back. And the worst thing was, I couldn't think of any reason why. Why would Brian make fun of me?

Lacey was speechless for a minute, but she recovered. "Mike Kalb didn't say anything mean about Kristin, did he?" she asked.

Naturally, that was the million-dollar question.

Annie looked at her friends, apparently trying to remember. "No, I don't think so," she said finally.

Brian appeared then, heading back to the booth from the pay phone. "There he is," Lacey told the others in a low voice.

"We have to get going anyway," Tara said. Janine and Annie grabbed their drinks and scooted out of the booth.

"We'll see you guys later," Janine said. "Nice meeting you, Kristin."

"Same here." I tried to sound as perky as possible and waved as they left the restaurant.

Kristin

As soon as the door closed behind them, Lacey turned to me. "Maybe it's for the best," she said quickly, squeezing my arm. "Now you'll listen to me. Concentrate on Mike." She glanced at Brian as he slid in across from us.

"Hi, Lacey," he said.

She glared at him. Brian was oblivious, as usual.

I watched him from the corner of my eye, feeling slightly sick to my stomach. Could this be the same Brian I'd known for so long? Had I completely misjudged him? Or had he turned on me? And why? None of it made any sense.

It's because I insulted him, I told myself, even though it seemed pretty hard to believe. *It has to be that.* I stole another glance at him. He was telling Lacey about the horror festival, comparing all his favorite movie monsters.

It's my fault, I told myself. *Brian wouldn't act this way for no reason. And that means it's up to me to find a way to apologize.*

Jessica

Monday, 3:12 P.M.

Dear Diary,

I am bored.

Bored, bored, bored, bored, bored.

Bored.

Derob. That's bored backward because I am beyond bored.

Do you know what is so messed up? I threw this huge, awesome party, right? And now people have started talking to me at school and coming up to me in the halls and stuff. And some of them have even started calling me. Like Kristin Seltzer— one of the coolest girls at SVJH—actually called to say hi last night *and my mother told her that I couldn't come to the phone because I was grounded!*

I mean, do they give parents lessons in how to humiliate kids before they're allowed to give birth? Or what?

That's life living in Dork City.

And now Elizabeth is making it worse by moping around and doing her homework all the

Jessica

time. All I have to say is that I hope Mom and Dad don't think that I'm going to start doing my homework all the time or something. Keep dreaming.

Not that there's much else to do.

I think I'll go do my nails.

Elizabeth

Dear Diary,

I had a great day at school. I've decided to concentrate on schoolwork—so I went to the library during lunch and stayed after all of my classes to ask for extra credit.

I'll bet I get all A's this semester.

And I'll never have to deal with my friends.

I wonder if Mom and Dad would consider grounding me forever.

Salvador

Dear Diary,
Is it possible to smother yourself to death with a pillow?

Elizabeth didn't talk to me all day.

She definitely thought my kiss was slimy.

A n n a

Dear Diary,

Is it my imagination, or was Elizabeth avoiding me all day?

She only talked to me long enough to let me know that she'd been grounded and that we couldn't have a 'zine meeting for two weeks.

Ohmigosh. I just thought of something. What if Elizabeth decided that my poem to Tim is terrible and doesn't know how to tell me? What if she doesn't want it to go in the 'zine after all? What if she's just putting off the 'zine meeting until she can find a kind way to tell me that my writing stinks?

I can't even think about this now. I'll just ask her tomorrow.

Lacey

"Go, go, go, go, gogogogogogogogo!" Gel shouted, and high-fived one of his dumb friends. The blond one. Eric.

It was another thrilling Monday night in Gel's basement. Gel and three of his friends were on the air-hockey machine, playing doubles. I was on the couch, reading *Vogue*.

I hate *Vogue*, but what was I supposed to do? Watch their stupid game? It was bad enough that I had to listen to it.

For about the millionth time I wished that Kristin were with me. Ever since I'd found out that was even a possibility, I could hardly stand hanging with Gel and his friends anymore. When I first started dating Gel, I thought it would be cool to hang with his older friends.

Then I realized that his friends weren't that cool. Except for Mike, of course. But at least high schoolers can drive and they have an easier time buying cigarettes and stuff.

But if Kristin were here, hanging in this smelly basement might actually be fun.

She and I had been friends since second grade. I never had to explain things to her like I did to other people—Kristin always understood where I was coming from. Kristin gets it, you know?

She's my one true friend. Everyone else is a Kleenex, as far as I'm concerned. As in, disposable.

"Hey, Lace," Gel shouted as he whacked the air-hockey puck. "Would you go get us some snacks?"

Speaking of disposable. I glared at Gel, but he was too busy playing air hockey to notice. I sighed and slapped the *Vogue* facedown on the couch. Normally I would have told Gel to get his own snacks, but I didn't mind escaping the basement for a little while. I stomped upstairs as loudly as I could, though, just so he would know I wasn't happy about being his servant.

Again I thought about Kristin. Mike Kalb wasn't at Gel's tonight, but he was often enough. If Mike and Kristin were here, the four of us would be on the air-hockey machine. Or Kristin and I would talk the guys into going out for a movie instead. Then my life would be tolerable.

I grabbed a big bag of chips and a jar of salsa. Then I got a six-pack of Coke out of the fridge and headed downstairs.

"You're the best, babe!" Gel said as I heaped

everything onto the air-hockey table. I just rolled my eyes at him. The other guys grabbed the food without even saying thanks. Not that I expected them to suddenly stop acting like pigs on my account. Eric took a sip of soda and let out a loud belch.

"This is really great!" Gel was talking with his mouth full, making bits of chip fly everywhere. Very appealing. "Don't you want any, Lacey?"

"No thanks," I said. "I'm not hungry."

I flopped back on the couch and picked up *Vogue.*

Kristin's date with Mike has to go well, I thought. *I'll make sure it does—even if it kills me.*

Kristin

I pulled the sweatshirt over my head just as Lacey appeared in the SVJH girls' room on Tuesday afternoon. I'd dashed to change my clothes the minute the final bell rang. It was all part of my brilliant master plan.

"Kristin!" Lacey gaped at me. "Don't!"

"Don't what?" I asked. I turned to study my reflection in the mirror. Perfect. The faded gray sweatshirt I'd borrowed from my dad years ago hung off me like a baggy old sack.

"You can't wear that," Lacey declared, staring at my outfit in disbelief. "Have you gone insane? What do you think you're doing?"

"Getting ready for a basketball game," I told her, grinning.

"You look terrible!" Lacey eyed me with growing horror. "That sweatshirt is disgusting—it totally hides your body! And those pants. Where did you get them? Out of some garbage can?"

"Don't you like them?" Teasing, I held out the

sides of my oldest pair of cargo pants. Each leg was about three feet wide. They were from this stage I went through a while ago when I took the whole oversized-clothes thing a little too seriously.

I spun around to give Lacey the full effect. She seemed ready to have a heart attack.

"Why are you doing this?" Lacey wailed. "You looked so great all day."

I had to admit, I *did* look pretty good today. I wore my favorite black flared jeans and a pink, zip-front top. The outfit made me look positively slender. I felt great in it from the moment I first tried it on. Some clothes are like that— they just make you feel terrific. And then there are the clothes that make you want to break down crying in the dressing room. But that's another story.

"Wait," I told Lacey. "You haven't seen the finishing touch." I pulled a battered red baseball cap out of my backpack and stuck it on my head backward. I grinned at Lacey.

"No. Absolutely not," she told me, lunging toward the hat.

I backed away from her and laughed. "Don't you get it?" I asked.

Lacey gave me a blank look.

"It's for Brian," I told her. "To apologize for making fun of his outfit. At the party Saturday night," I added when Lacey's look went from blank to confused.

"Are you serious?" Lacey asked.

"Totally," I answered. "I want him to see me wearing these baggy clothes. Then he'll know I didn't mean to insult his baggy clothes on Saturday night."

Lacey looked doubtful. "If you ask me, he should be trying to make you feel better."

I crossed my arms over my chest. "Whatever. I just want to make up," I told her.

"You can't walk around the school dressed like that," Lacey said. "Why don't you just take a picture and show it to him?"

"School is over anyway—it's not like tons of people will see me. And besides, this is the only way," I declared. "I have to do this in public. It won't make the same impression if I just show him some photograph."

"I don't understand why you care about him anyway," Lacey murmured. "I sure wouldn't go embarrassing myself for Brian Rainey."

"It won't be so bad," I reassured her. Actually, I thought the whole gag was pretty hilarious. Brian would think so too.

Lacey sighed. "Where are you supposed to meet Brian?"

"Nowhere. I mean, we don't have a date to

meet. But I know he's playing basketball after school today. Just a pickup game with some of the guys."

"Good. At least nobody important will see you, then," Lacey said. "Even me seeing you is one person too many," she added under her breath.

"I can stand looking a little weird if it makes things okay with Brian," I told her.

Lacey gave me a dubious look.

I tried not to smile. Lacey is one of those girls who really care about how they look. I think it's kind of hard for her to understand how other people have days when they look less than their best.

"So things with Brian are still funky?" Lacey asked.

"Yeah," I admitted. "He pretty much avoided me in the halls all day. And when I tried to sit near him at lunch, he made up some lame excuse about a stomachache."

Actually, he dumped his entire, uneaten, double taco supreme (his absolute favorite meal) in the trash and backed away from me. He said he was going to the nurse's office. But I doubted that. I personally know he hasn't set foot in the nurse's office since second grade. It's some warped male-pride thing with him.

I spent the whole afternoon thinking about it. It was pretty horrible, having him treat me that way. I guess you never know how much you're going to miss your friends until something like this happens. Thank goodness I still had Lacey.

"I've got to make this up to him somehow," I told her. "I can't take much more of the silent treatment." I took one last look in the mirror, then slung my backpack over my shoulder and headed for the door.

Lacey squared her shoulders. "Hang on, Kris. I'll come with you. Not that I care about you making up with Brian," she added. "I still think he's a jerk. But I'm always happy to watch cute guys play basketball." I shook my head. Lacey liked to act cooler than thou, but I knew she was doing this for me because she cared.

We walked out to the basketball courts together, talking about small stuff. Lacey kept glancing at me out of the corner of her eye and biting her lip.

Good, I thought. *That means my outfit makes exactly the right impression.*

Brian and a bunch of his friends were already spread over the court, doing practice layups. As we got closer, they grouped into teams and two players shot free throws to see who got the ball.

Lacey and I sat on the bleachers to watch.

"For a pickup game they're pretty serious," Lacey remarked, eyeing one of the sweaty, bare-chested guys.

"Tell me about it." I was surprised too. These guys meant business. The defensive players were practically beating up on the other guys. And the offense was in take-no-prisoners mode.

I called out to Brian and waved both my arms in the air. "Go, Rainey!" I yelled. He nodded my way, but that was it.

"Brian seems really focused," Lacey remarked.

"Yeah," I agreed. "And this isn't even a real game." That gave me an idea. "I'm going to do a cheer for Brian!"

"Oh no." Lacey groaned and rolled her eyes.

I ignored her. I'm on the cheer squad, and I know that having someone rooting you on can make a big difference.

One of his teammates hit Brian with a crisp bounce pass. I did a round of a cheer I'd made up last year called Make It Rain, and Brian hit a long-range jump shot from downtown.

"Whoo!" I shouted. "Rain on, Rainey!" Then I did my best hurkey.

Lacey rolled her eyes again. "Kristin, you and your cheerleading jumps—" She stopped suddenly. "Oh no! Look!" she said, jumping up and grabbing my arm. I glanced over at the opposite side of the court.

And gulped.

Billy Rainey was standing there, clapping for

Brian. And next to him stood Mike Kalb.

Mike was wearing old jeans and a soccer shirt. A dark blue shirt that made his eyes seem really intense. His hair was ruffled by the wind, and he was smiling and yelling.

He looked about a thousand percent adorable.

He caught me staring at him, and I suddenly realized how I looked. Like I just raided the thrift shop on baggy-clothes day. I groaned. Not again!

Lacey got it right away. "Do something," she whispered.

I whipped off the baseball cap. I wished I could whip off my sweatshirt and baggy pants too, but that was hardly possible.

"Smile," Lacey hissed at me. "At least smile. And sit down. Your outfit won't show so much."

I did what she said. Lacey sat next to me.

"How's my hair?" I asked out of the corner of my mouth. "Is it totally weird looking?"

"Smooth it down in the back," Lacey hissed. "It's all messed up from that dumb hat."

I quickly smoothed my hair. Why, oh why, did Mike have to show up when I looked this way? I could hardly stroll over there and tell him it was all a joke. He'd think I was a total loser.

Instead I sucked in my stomach for all I was worth. I pinned my arms to my sides too, tucking back the sweatshirt so it looked less baggy. I sat up as tall as I could and tried to look full of enthusiasm—anything to look less dumpy.

"How long have they been there?" I asked Lacey.

"I don't know. Not long, I think." Lacey let out a little moan. "I cannot believe your luck. This is such a total disaster."

"It's not that bad," I told her. "I mean, I probably look better than I did Saturday night. At least there's no red goop dripping down my face."

"At the very least," Lacey said. I could tell she was about to die. "Oh, great. Here they come."

It was true. Billy and Mike were walking toward us.

"Hi, guys," Billy said as he and Mike climbed up onto the bleachers behind us.

"Hi, Kristin," Mike said. He looked from me to Lacey. "Hey, Lacey. I didn't know you knew Kristin."

"We're best friends," Lacey said, flipping her hair over her shoulder.

A look of surprise flickered across Mike's face. Then it was gone. "No kidding."

We sat in silence for a moment, watching the game. I felt pretty awkward. I wanted to casually bring up my outfit and the fact that I don't usually dress as though I'm wearing a parachute, but I couldn't come up with anything that wouldn't sound bizarre.

"So, Kristin," Mike said, breaking the silence. "Are you going to do any more cheers for us?"

"Oh," I said casually, "I get enough of that in real games." Of course, really I just didn't want to stand up in my hideous outfit.

"Are you a cheerleader?" Mike looked kind of surprised again.

I nodded and smiled.

"She's cocaptain of the squad," Lacey said. That struck me as kind of funny because Lacey usually says that cheering is a waste of time. And here she was—practically bragging about it.

Just then Brian got fouled and had to go to the free-throw line. He glanced our way as he bounced the ball to line up his shot. He frowned at us, but I guessed he was just concentrating.

"Go, Brian!" I yelled.

Brian let the ball fly. And missed.

He shook his head.

"You can do it!" I yelled as he lined up his second shot. He let it go. Another air ball. Brian never misses a free throw—what was wrong with him today?

"Looks like I should be giving my brother a few basketball tips," Billy remarked.

"Spare me, Billy," I said. "You throw up so many bricks, you need a builder's permit."

Mike's eyes widened—then he gave a deep

belly laugh. "Did you hear that?" he said to Billy. "What a dis!" Then he grinned at me. "Are you into basketball, Kristin?"

"I love it," I said. "Rodman's my favorite."

Mike lifted his eyebrows. "Rodman? Really? Why?"

I shrugged. "Because he isn't perfect. He grabs all of those rebounds, but he can't shoot the ball. Plus he's a big, scary freak."

Mike laughed again, and I felt myself relax. Lacey gave me a little nudge with her elbow, as if to say, Nice save. No doubt about it, this was going pretty well in spite of my outfit. In fact, the way Mike was smiling at me made me feel positively beautiful.

Out on the court Brian dribbled the ball off his foot. But one of his teammates managed to grab it and score the final point.

Billy and Mike whooped and ran onto the court to slap high fives all around.

Ordinarily I would have run out there myself. But not today. "Let's go," I whispered to Lacey. Both of us raced for the school door. I beat Lacey to the girls' room and tore off my baggy clothes. I changed back into my cool outfit in record time.

"I hope Mike is still out there to see you looking like this," Lacey said.

We nearly tripped each other, racing to get back outside again.

But the court was empty. Billy and Mike were gone.

"Great," Lacey muttered sarcastically.

"It's not a total loss," I said, trying to look on the bright side. "At least I patched things up with Brian."

I glanced toward the side of the building. Brian was there, doing a postgame play-by-play with Salvador del Valle and a couple of other guys.

"Brian!" I called. Pulling Lacey along behind me, I hurried over to him. I saw Brian flash Salvador a desperate look before he peeled away from the group.

"Great game," I said when we reached Brian.

"Great," Lacey echoed.

"Thanks." Brian nodded and glanced away from me, shifting from one foot to the other.

Somehow I'd expected things to be back to normal. It threw me that Brian was still uncomfortable. For a minute I wasn't sure what to say next.

"So, how did you like your personal cheering squad?" I finally asked.

"Oh yeah. Right." Brian gave me a silly grin. "You were doing your cheerleader number."

Lacey nudged me in the side.

"Right," I said brightly. "But what I really want to know is, what did you think of my outfit?"

He stared at me. "Uh—it's great," he said.

61

"No, not this outfit," I said. "I mean, the outfit I had on before."

"Huh?" he said.

"You didn't notice my sweatshirt or anything?" I asked.

He seemed more uncomfortable than before. "No, but I'm sure it was really cute. You always look good—you know I think that, right?"

I couldn't believe it. He had no idea what I was talking about! Brian was totally living in oblivion! He never even noticed the baggy clothes.

"That's not what she meant at all, Brian," Lacey said in an impatient voice. "She wore this hideous outfit because of you, and—"

"Forget it," I interrupted. "Really," I told Lacey, giving her a drop-it look.

"What?" Brian asked.

"Nothing," I told him. "It wasn't important."

"Okay. Listen, I'd better go," Brian said. "See you around."

I watched him cut across the lawn, hurrying as if he couldn't wait to get away from me.

I didn't know whether to laugh or cry. "So I humiliated myself for nothing." I couldn't believe it. "He has no idea I was trying to make up with him."

Lacey threw up her hands. "Forget about Brian," she told me. "I'm more worried about Mike. First he sees you wearing party punch.

Then you show up in those awful baggy clothes. If I were him, I'd cancel the date."

"You wouldn't," I said, feeling alarmed.

"Why not?" Lacey asked. She frowned, looking grim. "We have to do some fast damage control."

"But he seemed to like talking to me—"

"Talking is fine," Lacey said, looking me in the eye. "For friends. But it isn't enough for a date."

"What can I do?" I felt totally clueless. Not a plan in my head. "Lacey, help! I've got to do something. Anything!"

Lacey nodded, apparently thinking. "No problem," she declared. "When in doubt, go shopping."

"Shopping?" I repeated.

"Sure. Tomorrow, right after school," she said.

"Maybe I'm dense," I said slowly. "But I don't see how shopping is going to save me."

"Trust me." Lacey grabbed my arm, and we turned toward home. "If shopping isn't the way to fix this situation, then I don't know anything about guys." She paused. "And I do know something about guys. True?"

"True," I admitted. I shrugged. I knew Lacey well enough not to argue. Besides, I was desperate. And if she said she could fix things, I was definitely going to believe her.

Salvador

Dear Diary,

Elizabeth did say hello to me today. We hung at her locker for about ten seconds, but then Anna came up, and everyone acted all uncomfortable until I finally gave up and went to Spanish. It ruined my whole day.

I was in such a lousy mood that not even the sight of Kristin Seltzer doing cheers in a hideous outfit at my after-school basketball game could make me feel better.

Anna

Dear Diary,

I was going to ask Elizabeth what she really thought about my poem when I saw her by her locker this morning, but she was standing with Salvador and acting really uncomfortable, so I chickened out.

Maybe Salvador knows something. I'll try to get him to tell me tomorrow.

Elizabeth

Tuesday, 3:28 P.M.

Dear Diary,

Algebra is starting to seem kind of fun.
Does that mean I'm losing it?

66

Brian

Wednesday. I stared at the word up on the board. How could it possibly be Wednesday already? There were only two days left before the Doggie Chow, and—as far as I knew—Kristin was still going. I kept bugging Billy to get Mike to cancel, and Billy kept promising that he would, but it hadn't happened yet. I was starting to worry that it might not happen at all. And then what would I do?

I couldn't believe Billy wasn't coming through for me. It just wasn't like him.

Could I find a way to warn Kristin? I was having a lot of trouble looking her in the eye these days. Not to mention talking to her. I just felt so guilty every time I thought about how this whole thing was my fault. What could I ever say to Kristin that could make it up to her?

"Five more minutes, people!" Mr. Delroyo, my algebra teacher, tapped the long, wooden pointer against his desk. "Make sure you double-check those answers," he said. "I know it's fashionable nowadays to concentrate on how you work out the problems," he added with a grin. "But I like to see the right answers too— once in a while."

A couple of kids chuckled at that. I barely cracked a smile. This whole date thing had me really messed up. I never realized before how much Kristin and I hung together—or how much it would bug me not to see her as much.

I looked back down at my quiz. *Concentrate,* I told myself. But the numbers looked like a foreign language. Nothing made sense. All I could think about was Kristin.

I wanted to put the whole date thing out of my mind, like my brother said. But it was amazingly tough. Like, today at lunch Salvador brought in one of those instant lunch packs with crackers and onion dip.

Kristin loves onion dip. And onion dip is something people eat at parties. Then I started to wonder whether she would eat onion dip at the Doggie Chow and . . .

"Mr. Rainey? Mr. Rainey!"

"Wha—" I bolted up in my seat. Then I peered around. The classroom was empty.

Mr. Delroyo was watching me, amused.

"Time's up," Mr. Delroyo said.

"Sorry!" I said, grabbing my stuff. I turned in my quiz and shot out the door.

"Hey, Rainey!" Salvador was waiting by the door as I entered the hall. A few of the guys I usually hang out with were there too. Salvador jabbed me with an elbow. "Trying to get a few brownie points in there?"

They all laughed.

"Funny," I said.

He grinned at me, but I couldn't smile back. "Want to shoot some hoops later?" he asked.

"Not today," I told him. "There's something I've got to do."

I left them and headed toward my locker. *All this thinking about Kristin isn't helping anything, I decided. I need to act normal with her, then I need to get on Billy's back and make him talk to Mike. That's it. No more acting weird. No more standing by and waiting for things to get better. So what if this whole situation is my fault? I just need to fix it, that's all. Starting now.*

Kristin's locker was around the corner from mine. If I hurried, I could catch her before she left for home.

"Kristin!" I rushed up to her open locker, where she was searching for a book inside. She seemed really surprised to see me, which made sense, considering I'd spent most of the week running away from her. "Uh, listen. We got this great new video game at home," I began, talking fast. "So, do you want to come over and try it out? I'll let you beat me at least once." I flashed my most charming grin.

Kristin blinked. "What are you talking about?"

"Global Domination," I told her. "That's the game. It's fun. Really."

She hesitated. "I don't know, Brian. I'm supposed to meet Lacey at the mall later. Besides—"

"Besides what?" I cut in before she gave me too many reasons not to come. Now that I was trying to patch things up, nothing was going to stop me. "No excuses," I said. "You can't pass this up. We've got plenty of diet soda. And my mom made those little cheese-snack things you love."

She thought about it for a minute, and for a second I was afraid she might say something like, "No, and by the way, I don't really want to be your friend anymore. . . ."

"All right," she said finally. "But only for a little while."

"Great!" I said, grinning my head off. "This is totally great."

"This is totally horrible!" I wailed forty minutes later. We were on our third game, and Kristin was demolishing my side of the world with radiated laser beams.

Zap!

"You lose again!" Kristin crowed in triumph. "Where have you been playing lately— kindergarten?"

"Don't rub it in," I told her. But I couldn't help smiling. *See how well this is working?* I told myself. It was great to be back to normal. I just hoped it would last.

"Brian," she said, "I want you to know that I'm sorry."

Sorry? Kristin didn't have anything to be sorry for. "About what?" I asked.

"You know," she said, looking down at her hands. "About the clothes thing."

I was about to ask her what she was talking about when a door banged downstairs. Billy was home. A second later I heard him whistling and slamming cabinet doors. *He sounds like he's in a pretty good mood,* I thought. *Maybe he finally got Mike to break the date! That would be so great. See? Everything is falling into place.*

Kristin glanced at her watch. "One more game?" she asked.

I gave her a slow blink. "I thought you were in a hurry to meet Lacey."

"There's plenty of time," she said, tossing back her head. "It'll only take about thirty seconds for me to annihilate you."

71

"I'm not afraid of you," I said in my best tough-guy voice. "But I am hungry. Do you want a snack?" Actually, I wasn't hungry at all. I just wanted to get downstairs and talk to Billy.

"Bring those little cheese things," Kristin called after me.

I ran downstairs to the kitchen. Billy was practically pulling the refrigerator apart, searching for food. He eats like a horse.

"Where's the rest of the taco stuff?" Billy called over his shoulder. "I'm having a major snack attack."

"I don't know." I lowered my voice. "Listen, did you talk to Mike yet?"

"There's nothing to drink either!" Billy was on his knees, feeling around the back of the refrigerator.

"Billy. This is important," I said. "Forget your stomach for two seconds, would you?"

"What?" Billy stood up, holding a carton of milk, a container of cold cuts, and a jar of mayonnaise. He dumped it all on the table and grabbed a loaf of bread and an enormous bag of potato chips.

"The date," I told him. "Did you get Mike to break his date with Kristin? I've only been asking you about it every day this week," I added.

Billy looked annoyed. "Would you quit bugging me? I said I'd try." He started stacking ham and cheese onto two slabs of bread.

"Well?" I prodded. "Did you?"

"Yeah." Billy stopped what he was doing for a minute and looked at me. "I asked him yesterday, Brian. He said no."

"What?" My legs went numb, and I felt dizzy. I grabbed the table for support.

"Mike said no," Billy repeated quietly. "He said it's too late."

"No, it isn't," I shrieked. "It's only Wednesday!"

"He tried, Brian," Billy told me. "But he couldn't find another date. It's too last minute. Look, if it makes you feel any better, Mike really wants to back out. He just can't."

"Someone would go," I insisted. "Anyone."

"No one," Billy said. "There's nothing he can do about it, okay?"

"No, it's not okay!" My voice was starting to rise. "It's absolutely, totally not okay. I told you, I don't want Kristin to go on that date! You were supposed to—"

"What's going on?"

I felt a tingle go down my spine. Really. I know that's a cliché, but I swear, at the sound of Kristin's voice behind me, I felt this tingling sensation race from my brain down the whole length of my back. It was sort of like fear. Only worse.

I can't describe the look she had on her face when I turned around.

"Whoa. I'm out of here." Billy grabbed his

food and started to bolt up to his room, even though we're not supposed to eat upstairs.

"Wait, Billy," Kristin said. "I want to know what Brian asked you to do."

Billy shot me a look that said he did not want to be involved.

"What are you doing in here?" I asked her before Billy replied. I knew it was a lame thing to say, but I don't think fast in situations like this.

"I thought I'd help you get the food." Kristin paused. "I heard everything you said," she added. Then her chin started to wobble, and her eyes filled with tears. "Why are you doing this?"

"I'm not!" I insisted. "I mean, it isn't . . . it isn't . . ." I had absolutely no idea what to tell her.

She stared at me a minute, then turned and walked away without a word. I heard the front door slam.

I turned to face my brother. "Thanks a lot, Billy," I said.

"What did I do?" Billy looked offended.

"I'm going after her," I said. I tried to brush past him, but he grabbed my arm and held me.

"Hang on!" Billy glared at me. "What are you going to tell her?"

I stared at him. "What do you think I'm going to tell her?" I demanded. "I'm going to tell her the truth."

"No way." Billy poked me in the chest. "You're not the only one who matters," he told me angrily. "What about Mike? This so-called date is like a major, major deal for him. He needs to do this to get into the order. He really wants to get in."

"I know, but—"

"Listen, Brian. It's all up to you." Billy let go of my arm and backed off. "Are you going to blow this for Mike?"

I sighed. It was too confusing. "I don't know," I admitted.

"Think about it," Billy went on. "Sure, it's rough for Kristin. But it all comes down to one date. She can get over one bad date. But Mike's entire social life could be ruined. Four years of high school down the drain. Out of the order for good. Is that fair to him?"

"When you put it that way, no," I said.

"Right," Billy said. "And what about me? Three years without my best friend, sharing my best times? And what about you, Bri? Don't you want to pledge the order when you get to high school?"

I thought about it. "Yeah," I admitted.

"Don't let me down, little bro." Billy punched me lightly on the arm. "Rainey brothers rule— remember that. I know you want to help your friend, but you can't be selfish about this."

Brian

I looked at Billy. I knew he didn't want to hurt Kristin's feelings any more than I did. Billy was right, as usual. In a way, it was three against one: Mike, Brian, and me against Kristin. Like Billy said, she'd be miserable, but only for one night.

"You're right," I finally said. "I can't tell her."

Sal—
Do you think Elizabeth is acting kind of strange?
                                    Anna

~~Why, do you? No.~~ Maybe. Why would she be?
                                    Salvador

I don't know. Has she said anything to you?
                                    A.

Why? Has she said anything to you?
                                    Salvador

Is there something you want to tell me?
                                    A.

Did Elizabeth tell you to ask me that?
                                    Sal

Forget it!
I'm sorry I asked.

Elizabeth

Wednesday, 5:07 P.M.

Dear Diary,

Jessica is acting strange. Honestly, I'm a little worried about her.

Every day when we come home from school, she spends at least two hours in the bathroom that connects our rooms. I'm not exaggerating.

Today, after two hours and fifteen minutes of listening to her hum in there, I knocked on the door. Aside from the fact that her humming was distracting me from my homework and I wanted her to cut it out, I also had to use the toilet.

Finally after I'd banged on the door for about five minutes, Jessica poked her head out. Her hair was in about a thousand tiny braids.

Diary, I swear, all I said was, "Those braids are against the school dress code." But Jessica totally flipped out, called me a goody-goody, and slammed the door in my face. I had to use the bathroom down the hall.

Can you believe that?

Lacey

"Kristin!" I called when I saw her walking toward me. I was standing by the fountain in the lower level of the mall—it's where we always meet. In fact, I had been standing there for ten minutes already. Kristin was late, and I was ready to hear my apology.

Kristin walked right past me.

Excuse me? "Kristin!" I shouted. This time she nearly jumped out of her skin. She whirled around to face me.

"Lacey!" she gasped. "What are you trying to do? Give me a heart attack?"

I rolled my eyes. "Didn't you see me waving at you?" I demanded.

"No, I . . . no. Sorry," she said. She was looking around like she wasn't sure where she was or something. She seemed pretty distracted, and I figured there was no point in making this into a big scene. Besides, I was really psyched to find Kristin a totally gorgeous outfit for the date of the millennium.

"No biggie," I said. "Let's go get you some clothes."

Kristin just shrugged. *Why is she so down?* I wondered. I decided it was because she hates shopping. One time when we went looking for bathing suits, Kristin ended up sobbing in the dressing room. We were in a department store with awful lighting—so of course Kristin looked terrible in everything. Both of us did. But Kristin really freaks out about her weight sometimes. Most of the time she pretends she doesn't care, but I know her stupid mother—Margie—puts a lot of pressure on her to lose weight. She tried to send Kristin to a fat camp once, and Kristin cried for a week.

I could've killed Margie for that.

But there wasn't going to be any sobbing in the dressing room today. We were going to find the hottest outfit on the planet, and Kristin was going to look incredible—no matter what. *This date is too important,* I thought. *Kristin has to look just*— Suddenly my eye fell on a store display. "Stop! Look at this!"

I grabbed Kristin's arm and dragged her over to the window of Romantique, a shop we usually don't bother with. Too expensive. And the salespeople watch every move you make—as if I would try to take something from a store like that anyway. But the dress in the window was It. I just knew it.

"There it is," I told Kristin. "That's what you need."

Kristin looked skeptical. "Which one?" she asked.

Wasn't it obvious? "The mannequin in the corner," I replied.

"The one in the bright red slip?" she asked. "What about it?"

"She looks like you," I explained patiently.

"Like me?" She looked at the mannequin again, then started to laugh. "That mannequin is twelve feet tall and weighs about two pounds. She looks about as much like me as Arnold Schwarzenegger does."

I rolled my eyes. "You don't get it," I said. "You're looking at tiny details. I'm talking about something else."

Kristin looked blank. "Like what?" she asked.

Is Kristin going for the Spiritless Award or something? I wondered. Anyone would think that this date was more important to me than to her. "Like the way she holds herself. Her attitude." I studied the mannequin. It was the color of the dress that worked so well—it would look great with Kristin's hair. And Kristin had a pair of sandals very close to what the mannequin was wearing. No doubt about it—we could make this work.

"You're insane," Kristin declared. "Mannequins don't 'hold themselves.'"

I groaned. "You're just being stubborn," I said. "She looks like you, trust me."

"Right." Kristin pointed to a male mannequin in the window of a neighboring store. "And I suppose this guy looks like Gel. Or Mike."

I looked across at the blond mannequin. "Actually," I said, "he looks more like Brian."

Kristin frowned and didn't say anything.

"Laugh," I ordered. "I'm trying to cheer you up. You're supposed to be loving every minute of this shopping trip."

"If you want me to cheer up, don't talk about Brian," Kristin said darkly.

"Here we go." I folded my arms across my chest. "I knew something was wrong. What did he do now?"

Kristin sighed. "I overheard him talking to Billy. Brian was saying that Billy should make Mike break his date with me."

What? Was Brian overdosing on jerk vitamins? "He is so dead," I said.

"Lacey, please," Kristin begged. "Don't get involved."

"So, did Billy actually talk to Mike about it?" I asked.

Kristin frowned. "I'm trying to remember. I

think he did," she said slowly. "I heard Billy say something about how it was too late for Mike to ask someone else."

"This is unbelievable!"

"And then Brian kind of went crazy," Kristin went on. "He started yelling at Billy, saying he didn't want me to go on the date." Kristin shook her head.

"Oh, Kristin," I said, and gave her a hug. No wonder she couldn't get psyched for shopping— the whole date had practically been called off! "Well, forget about Brian," I said as I pulled away. "Who knows why he's acting so weird? Just don't let him get to you. You have more important things to worry about." I looked her in the eye. "After all, Mike didn't break the date, right?"

Kristin smiled a little then. I guess she knew I was right.

"But why is Brian doing this?" Kristin asked.

"I guess he doesn't want you to have a boyfriend," I suggested. "He's afraid you won't need him anymore."

"It's only one date," Kristin countered. "Besides, Brian and I are just friends."

"Yeah, but for how long?" I said. "Even Brian isn't that much of an idiot. He knows what a big deal this date is. He knows you'll be hanging with me more—with Mike's friends and mine.

You'll have a whole bunch of new people to spend time with. And they'll be in high school! Then maybe you'll have better things to do than come cheer for Brian's pickup basketball games or cross-country meets." I shook my head. "Brian is just acting like a jealous baby."

Kristin seemed to accept that answer. To be honest, I had no idea whether it was true or not. But it was as good an explanation as any, I supposed. I didn't say anything more about Brian as we stepped into Romantique. Neither did Kristin. I just hoped she was learning her lesson about him. The problem with Kristin is that she doesn't realize that she is way too cool for some people.

I began pawing through the racks.

No. No. No—bingo! "This is it," I said with finality. Kristin turned to look at what I'd found.

"Lacey, no!" Kristin said when she saw the bright red dress. "I told you, I'm not a mannequin."

"Just try it," I urged. "You're going to thank me."

Kristin rolled her eyes, grabbed it, and stomped over to the dressing room.

"I'll wait right here," I said as Kristin closed the door.

"Terrific," Kristin said without enthusiasm.

A few seconds later the door to Kristin's dressing room swung open.

"Are you satisfied?" she demanded.

I caught my breath. "You look amazing!" I said. "Come and look in the three way."

Kristin followed me over to the big mirror. When she finally bothered to look at her reflection, I could see she was pretty surprised. But I wasn't. She looked exactly how I always knew she could look.

"Twirl," I ordered.

She spun around obediently, craning her neck so she could see herself at every angle.

"That's it," I announced. "That dress is so hot, you could melt." She grinned. "Or Mike could melt," I added, cocking my right eyebrow.

Kristin flushed almost as red as the dress, but she was smiling.

The fabric was so smooth and satiny, it actually gleamed. The top clung, smooth fitting but not tight. It showed off Kristin's curves without being low cut. Kristin looked hot—but not like she was trying hard to do it.

Kristin flipped up the price tag. Her mouth dropped open in horror.

"Don't even," I said. "You're getting this dress if I have to steal it for you."

I gave Kristin a meaningful glance so that she would know I was only half kidding.

"That's okay," she said. "Mom gave me the credit card and told me I could get something really special for this dinner. So I think I'll just pay for it." She giggled and practically skipped back to the dressing room.

Kristin was humming the whole time we waited on line to pay for the dress. Usually that would have gotten on my nerves—but not today. When Kristin is happy, I'm happy. And when Kristin looks amazing for her date with Mike Kalb, I'm twice as happy.

We walked out of Romantique . . . and straight into Billy Rainey.

"Uh, hi," he said, looking uncomfortable. "What are you guys doing here?"

We're on the lookout for lame people to have boring conversations with, and we just hit the jackpot, I wanted to say. But I restrained myself. "We're buying a hot dress for Kristin's date with Mike," I said instead.

"Lacey!" Kristin looked mortified. She grabbed my arm and dragged me away.

"See you, Billy!" I called over my shoulder.

Kristin dragged me around the nearest corner. "Are you crazy?" she demanded. "Why did you say that?"

I sighed. "I just want those Raineys to know that they can't screw this up for you, that's all," I said. "Besides, what do you care if I told Billy that you're going to look great? It's the truth, isn't it?"

Kristin shrugged.

"Well, isn't it?" I demanded.

"I guess—," Kristin hedged.

"No," I cut her off. "You're going to look great. End of story. Now I want you to say it to yourself ten times every day. Starting right now."

Kristin giggled. "Okay, I give up. I'm going to look great."

I nodded. That was more like it. Mike and Kristin were going to have the best date in the history of humankind—even if I had to go on it myself.

Brian

Wednesday night means spaghetti at our house. That means a major cleanup after dinner. There are seven of us, and on Wednesday nights it feels like an army invaded our kitchen.

It's not too bad when everyone pitches in. Usually Billy and Ellie are in charge of putting all the leftovers away. They're the oldest, so for years they were the only ones who could reach the high cabinets. Ellie was *still* taller than Billy and me—and she never let us forget it.

The rest of us are on dish duty. I'm kind of unofficially in charge. Addie is eight and hyper; she breaks things a lot if you don't watch her. But Sam is twelve, and she's pretty careful. Sometimes we make a sort of assembly line from the kitchen table to the dishwasher. Addie clears, handing things to Sam. Sam passes them to me, and I load them into the dishwasher.

We all assumed our positions and started to clean up.

Billy turned to me with a sly grin. "Guess who I saw at the mall today?"

"How should I know?" I said. I grabbed a stack of plates from Addie before she could drop them.

"Give us a hint," Addie begged. She loves guessing games.

I loaded the plates into the dishwasher.

"Let's just say, a certain person Brian knows very well had just bought a really hot dress." Billy paused. "A dress she's saving for a certain very big date."

"Who? What big date?" Ellie asked, immediately interested.

I could feel my cheeks burning. I knew who he meant.

"Who is it?" Sam demanded.

"Guess." Billy struck an exaggerated pose, pretending to be a girl teetering around the kitchen on imaginary high heels. He strutted from corner to corner, batting his eyelashes and pouting.

Addie and Sam giggled at him. I wasn't laughing, though. In fact, I wanted to kill him. It made me sick to think about how happy Kristin was—and about how devastated she would be when she found out the truth. How could Billy joke about it? I thought he liked Kristin. How dare he make fun of her?

"Cut it out," I told Billy.

Brian

"What's going on?" Ellie asked me. She was smiling at Billy, but she wasn't teasing, like the others.

"Kristin has a date, that's all," I muttered.

"An important date," Billy corrected. "With a friend of mine."

"Who?" Ellie demanded.

"Mike Kalb," I said abruptly. "It's no big deal."

"Ooooh," Addie sang out, teasing. "Brian lost his girlfriend! Brian is jealous!"

Sam picked up the refrain, and the two of them started marching around the kitchen, chanting it over and over: "Brian lost his girlfriend! Brian lost his girlfriend!"

I wanted them to shut up, but I knew better than to say so. They'd keep it up twice as long if I paid any attention. I pretended to ignore them, arranging the plates in the dishwasher, even though I'd already arranged them.

Ellie stood close to me. "Is Kristin interested in him?" she asked in a low voice so the others couldn't hear.

I was grateful that someone wanted to talk about it in a serious way. But I couldn't really tell her everything I was thinking. Not with Billy and everyone else around. Besides, I couldn't tell Ellie about the Secret Order of the Golden Moose. I'd promised I would keep their secret.

"I don't know if she likes him. Maybe she does. I guess so," I told Ellie. "It's just one date."

Ellie gazed at me thoughtfully. "That explains it," she said.

"Explains what?" I asked.

"I knew I hadn't seen her around as much lately," Ellie said. "Well, don't get upset about it," she added. "I mean, you guys did hang out together a lot. And it's hard to lose a friend, especially in the beginning when they're all excited about a new boyfriend or girlfriend. I've been through that before. It's hard not to sulk."

Her voice was friendly, but it rubbed me the wrong way.

"I'm not sulking. It's not that way at all!" My voice was louder than I intended. Billy glanced up and gave me a long look.

"He doesn't want her to go," Billy said slowly.

I glared at him. "That's right—I don't."

"What do you mean?" Ellie asked. She turned to look at me again. "I thought you and Kristin were just friends. Do you mean there's more to it than that?"

"No. I mean, we were . . . are friends," I said. "That's not the problem. There is no problem," I added.

"Did you have a fight or something?" Ellie prodded.

"Yes. I mean, no." I stopped. I was getting flustered trying to explain about our fight without spilling the beans about the phony date. "I don't know. I can't exactly explain it."

"You're so cute when you're upset." Ellie reached out and ruffled my hair. I hate when she does that. "Hey, don't worry," she went on. "These things happen. But you're a really nice guy, Brian. You and Kristin will work it out."

"Brian and Kristin, sitting in a tree," Addie sang. *"K-i-s-s-i-n-g!"*

"Come on, let's go see what's on TV," Ellie said, herding Addie and Sam out of the kitchen. "Quiet, you guys," I heard her whisper as they disappeared.

I was glad they were gone. But not so glad to be left alone with Billy.

He smirked at me. "Don't look so glum. Lighten up."

"How do you expect me to do that?" I yelled. "Kristin is my friend—how can you be so cruel to her?"

"Why are you so hung up on her? Kristin's not worried about you," Billy pointed out. "She's having a great time shopping for the big event."

"Yeah, so Mike can make her feel even more like a loser! Don't you understand that it only makes me feel worse to think about how happy she is when I know how miserable she's going to be Friday night? I should be protecting her, not standing by and letting you make fun of her."

Billy ran his hand through his hair. "Don't start that again."

"Why not?" I demanded. "You're trying to protect Mike, aren't you? So why shouldn't I look out for my friend too?"

"The date will happen. It has to," Billy said. He sighed. "Look, let's not talk about it anymore. I'm sorry I brought it up."

I knew I should drop the subject, but I had to give it one last try. "All Mike needs to do—"

"Forget it!" Billy yelled. I must have looked upset because his expression suddenly softened. "C'mon, Bri—let it go."

"Kristin and I have been friends a really long time, Billy," I said. "I know her. If I let her go to this dinner, she'll never get over it. She'll hate herself for thinking a high-school guy could really want to go out with her. She'll start to think she really *is* ugly. She'll feel like a loser, and she won't trust the next guy who asks her out, and . . . and she'll never forgive me. Never."

"She'll get over it," Billy said. "You're blowing this way out of proportion."

I shook my head. "I can't do it. I have to tell her."

Billy was silent for a minute. When he spoke again, his voice was low but steady. "Fine. Tell her. But you have to realize that you're making a choice—her over me. And if you choose Kristin, things between you and me will never be the same."

"That's crazy!" I said. "How can you even say that? You're my brother."

"I know I'm your brother," Billy said. "I'm not the one who seems to have forgotten what that means."

I swallowed. Why did this have to be so difficult? Why couldn't Billy see my side?

"I can't choose between you guys," I told him.

"You're going to have to," Billy replied. "You have one day to figure it out. Whose side are you on? Kristin's? Or mine?"

Kristin

"Kristin!"

I spun around. Who was calling me?

I was headed to cheer squad after school on Thursday and couldn't think of anyone who might need to catch me before practice. For a split second I thought it must be Brian. But it didn't sound exactly like him. Then I spotted somebody sitting in a car. He was parked at the curb by the playing fields.

Mike?

I couldn't believe it. What was he doing here?

"Hey, Kristin—over here!" he called again, waving me over.

I hesitated. Naturally, he'd just caught me looking gross again! I had on this old navy sweat suit I wore only to cheering practice. It was faded, but at least it fit well. Not at all baggy.

And my hair was fine. I'd just brushed it when I changed for practice. Actually, I guess I looked pretty good except for the less than glamorous outfit.

Okay, so I didn't look gross. Still, I wished I looked better than okay.

I actually considered rushing back into the gym and changing into the outfit I'd worn to school. It was a really cute crop-top cardigan and tight-fitting jeans.

But that would be hard to explain. And what if Mike was gone when I got back?

"Kristin!" he called a third time. I smiled and waved back as I headed toward his car.

Had he really come to school to see me? And why? I mean, he could have called me yesterday and asked if he could meet me after school. At least that would have given me some warning.

Maybe he just had an impulse to see me again. Cool.

I tried not to grin like an idiot. I could hardly believe I was walking toward his car. I was suddenly very aware of everything around me.

Like the fact that Susie Chapman and Kelly Lit, a couple of younger girls on the cheering squad, were staring at me in total envy. The way I used to envy Lacey, hurrying somewhere to meet Gel.

Now I was just like her.

"Hey," Mike said as I reached the car. It was a nice, comfortable blue Honda. I guessed it was his parents' car, not his. He'd probably use it to pick me up for our date on Friday.

I felt a tingle of excitement.

"Hey," I greeted him with an especially big smile. Lacey always says my smile is one of my best features—that it lights up my whole face.

I guess it does. Because Mike's eyes kind of lit up when I smiled at him. It made me feel great.

"What's up?" I added when he didn't say anything more.

"Uh, nothing special," he answered. He looked kind of confused, actually.

"Should I get in?" I suggested, pointing at the car.

He looked even more embarrassed. "Sure," he said. "I mean, yeah. We should talk," he added.

I loved walking over to the passenger side of the car. I tried to do it really casually, as if this happened to me every day of the week. "Oh, my boyfriend dropped by to see me," I imagined myself telling the entire cheer squad. It felt great.

I slid in and shut the car door. "So, what should we talk about?" I asked.

He hesitated, then kind of shook his head. "Well . . . I don't know," he finally said.

"Me either," I told him. We both laughed. "I'm on my way to practice," I explained, gesturing toward my clothes.

"Cheer squad," he said. "Are you going to do some of the same cheers you did the other day?"

I cringed. "You know, I've been thinking about that day. Maybe I should explain about the clothes."

"Your clothes?" he repeated.

"Yeah. I don't usually wear baggy clothes," I explained. "It was kind of a complicated joke. On Brian," I added.

Mike looked blank. "I don't get it."

"Neither did Brian," I said, rolling my eyes.

Mike laughed. "You don't have to worry about your clothes with me," he said. "I barely even notice that kind of stuff. In fact, I totally spaced picture day and wore a gross ripped T-shirt to school—two years in a row. The same shirt!"

"Ohmigosh, I hate doing embarrassing stuff like that," I told him. "Two years ago I got this really small part in the school play. Well, since I only had a few lines to learn, I figured I didn't need to practice much. Then the day of the play, just as I was supposed to go onstage, I got this terrible case of stage fright!"

"That's happened to me too," Mike admitted.

"Usually I don't get nervous in front of people," I told him. "I guess that's why I can be on cheer squad and everything. But this time I totally forgot my lines. I suddenly had no idea what I was supposed to say. I completely froze. Someone shoved me onto the stage, and I tripped and fell into a huge piece of scenery. I knocked it over, and then all the rest of the scenery came crashing down!"

"No way." Mike was grinning.

"Oh yes," I told him. "Total disaster! The whole play had to be canceled." I heaved a dramatic sigh. "And all because I had a small part. If I'd had the lead, I would have rehearsed a ton and it never would have happened."

"Well, I hope they learned their lesson," Mike said. "Nothing but the lead for Kristin Seltzer!"

We smiled at each other.

Sara Carnes and Lindsey Warner passed the car, late to practice as usual. Sara waved when she saw us sitting together. Lindsey just stared. I tried to look like I hung out with cute high-school guys every day. Sara had to pull Lindsey away.

When I glanced back at Mike, I caught him studying me. He had a really strange look on his face. My heart thudded in my chest.

"Uh, Kristin," he said quietly. He stared at his hands. "Did you ever do anything really mean? And stupid?" he added, suddenly looking into my eyes.

"Sure," I said. "Everybody does stuff like that sometimes."

"But I mean something really stupid," Mike said. "What do you do if you realize you might be making a mistake, but you don't know how to fix it?"

I shrugged. "There's nothing that can't be fixed."

Mike shook his head, then he sighed and looked out the window. "You're so nice." His voice was far away, though, as if he wasn't really even talking to me.

His eyes were troubled. I felt so bad for him that I reached out and grabbed his hand. I don't usually do stuff like that—especially not with guys—but he looked so sad that I couldn't think of anything else to do. "You'll do the right thing," I told him.

He looked over at me. He glanced at my hair, then into my eyes, and smiled softly. It was sort of a sad smile. "How did this happen?" he asked.

I felt a little dizzy, and I realized I was holding my breath.

Mike was still staring at me, and we were still holding hands. He swallowed as if he had something more to say—something important.

"Hey, Mike! What's up, man?" Gel poked his head into the car through the open window. "Oh, hey, Kris." I drew back, startled. So did Mike. He dropped my hand.

Then I noticed Lacey standing behind Gel. Her eyes met mine, opening wide when she glanced at Mike sitting beside me. She lifted her eyebrows and smiled.

The spell was totally broken. Mike got out of the car and gave Gel a high five. "Gel! How's it going?"

I got out of the car too.

"I didn't know Mike was here," Lacey whispered to me.

"He wanted to talk, I guess," I whispered back.

Lacey squeezed my hand. "I'm glad he finally got to see the real you." She was smiling, and I felt like there was a big lightbulb inside me, totally lighting me up.

I glanced down at my sweat suit. "Practice!" I yelped. I'd almost forgotten it.

"Mike, I have to go," I called over to him. He glanced at Gel, then nodded.

"Catch you later," he said.

Lacey linked arms with me. "I'll walk you," she said. "Be right back," she told Gel.

We hurried across the field together. I could see the squad doing their opening warm-ups. I sped up.

"Slow down," Lacey told me. "I want to hear everything."

"Oh, Lacey," I began. "I think he was going to kiss me or something."

"What?" Lacey grinned. "Really?"

"Really," I said.

"Wow." Lacey stopped and stared at me. "That's so great, Kristin."

"Thanks," I said.

"It's all working out just the way I imagined," Lacey added. "You must be so excited."

"I really am," I admitted. "Mike is great. He's funny and nice and easy to talk to. I feel so lucky." I thought about the way Mike had been staring into my eyes and felt warm all over.

"I wonder if he'll call you tonight?" Lacey said.

"I hope so," I told her. "I don't know how I can stand waiting till Friday night to see him again."

"That's only tomorrow!" Lacey teased.

"I can't help it," I said. "I never liked any boy this way before."

Not even Brian, I added silently to myself. I'd spent years crushing on Brian, but that was totally different. I knew Brian so well, he was almost like a brother sometimes. But everything about Mike was new and exciting. The way he looked, the way he moved and talked. I was dying to spend every minute I could with him to get to know him better. Besides, Brian never made me feel like the prettiest girl in the room.

My crush on Brian seemed to have evaporated overnight. He'd pretty much cured me by acting so horrible lately. I actually felt sick when I remembered him trying to get Billy to break my date.

Mike would never do something like that.

I couldn't wait for tomorrow night. Mike would see me in my new dress, see me really dressed up for the first time.

And maybe tomorrow he really would kiss me!

A n n a

Dear Diary,

Today Elizabeth finally sat with me and Salvador at lunch, and all she could talk about was her stupid, annoying sister!

As if we didn't already know that Jessica is annoying.

Well, if Elizabeth isn't going to have the guts to tell me to my face that she doesn't like my poem, that's fine by me.

I'll just keep pretending that I don't realize what's going on. She'll either have to talk to me or print the poem.

Ha!

I hope she feels really guilty about this.

Salvador

Dear Diary,

Elizabeth still hasn't said word one about the kiss.

I guess she wants to pretend that it never happened.

And I guess I'll have to accept that.

Jessica

Thursday, 5:10 P.M.

Dear Diary of My Pathetic Life,

I can't stand one more minute of living with Little Miss Perfect!

Do you know what she did today? As if that "your hairstyle does not adhere to school policy" comment yesterday wasn't bad enough, Elizabeth actually tried to get me into trouble with Mom today!

I was using the computer, and she just came up to me and told me to stop! Elizabeth said that she had to do homework. Like her stuff is so much more important than mine!

So, of course, I was like, "No way," and she was like, "Get off," and I was like, "Forget it," and she was like, "Fine, I'm telling."

Like we're in first grade!

So finally I just said good-bye to everyone in the chat room and let precious Elizabeth do her social studies paper.

She's driving me crazy!

Brian

Nearly five o'clock on Friday.
D day.

D for deadline. *D* for Doggie Chow.

D for do something.

Billy would be home any minute. In fact, he should have been home already. I was not looking forward to seeing him. I managed to avoid him this morning. But I couldn't stop hearing his voice in my head. The way he sounded yesterday when he said I had to choose between him and Kristin.

How was I supposed to do that?

I gnawed the end of my pencil. I was supposed to be doing math homework. But I couldn't concentrate on math. I couldn't concentrate on anything. I'd spent the whole day acting like a zombie from planet Freakazoid. I even walked into the wrong class last period.

The fact was, any way you sliced it, I had to let someone down.

Brian

I knew that Billy was wrong. And that he was acting like a jerk. But Billy is my brother.

On the other hand, I couldn't let Kristin go on that date. Absolutely not.

But how could I warn her? I couldn't tell her now because she'd be furious that I let it go this long without telling her. Besides, she might not even believe me—she thought I'd been acting bizarre.

If only someone else would tell her, I thought, *that would solve everything.*

Wait—someone else! That's it! I leaped up and started pacing around my room.

I am a genius! Sometimes, that is. The answer was so obvious. Why hadn't I seen it before?

An anonymous letter! Sure, that was it. I could write to Kristin, explain the whole truth about the Doggie Chow, and not sign my name!

Beyond perfect. I mean, I wouldn't get any credit for trying to save her. But at least she'd be saved.

And Billy wouldn't have my head for it either. He wouldn't know I stabbed him in the back. Because no one would know who blabbed!

I tore out a fresh sheet of loose-leaf and grabbed my pen. No, wait. I took out a purple marker instead, figuring that would be more of a disguise. Oh—wait. I'd have to disguise my handwriting too.

That wasn't going to work—I can't even disguise my handwriting so that it looks decent, much less so that it looks like anything anyone else would write. I'd have to print it out on the computer. That was better anyway. Then it would be totally anonymous.

I raced down to the family room and turned on the computer. I hitched up my chair, grabbed the keyboard, and started typing.

Dear Kristin,
   You don't know me, but I have to warn you. Your date with Mike isn't a real date.

I read it over and frowned. It sounded kind of harsh. Maybe I should start off slowly.

I deleted the text and started again.

Dear Kristin,
   As your friend I tell you—beware of Friday night!

I rolled my eyes. Now I sounded like a fortune-teller in a low-budget movie.

Delete.

Dear Kristin,
   Mike doesn't really like you. He only asked you out because . . .

Because what? Because you looked so bad the other night, he thought you were a total beast?

Hold on, I told myself. *You can't mention that night anyway, or she'll know you wrote the letter. You, Billy, and Mike were the only ones who saw her with punch hair.*

Good save, Bri, I told myself.

Delete.

Kristin—I'm telling you this because I care about you. And Mike doesn't. He just wants to use you.

I cringed. Now I sounded jealous. Like some girl who wanted to scare Kristin off so she could have Mike to herself.

This letter was a lot harder to write than I thought it would be.

I deleted it again and ran my fingers through my hair. *Concentrate,* I thought, *concentrate, concentrate*—

"What's up?" Addie poked her head into the room, and I nearly jumped out of my chair.

"Don't sneak up on me like that!" I told her.

"Chill out, Brian," Addie told me. "What are you doing anyway? Playing Battleship?"

"No, I'm doing something important," I replied irritably. "And little sisters aren't invited."

Naturally, she came in and plopped down in the armchair next to the desk.

"What's so important?" she asked.

"Why was I cursed with little sisters?" I gave a dramatic groan. Addie giggled. "All right, I'll tell you if you promise to go away," I said.

"I promise." Addie leaned forward eagerly.

"Okay, then." I gestured toward the computer screen. "I'm trying to write a letter, but I can't get it to say exactly what I want to say."

"Is that all?" Addie sat back, clearly disappointed. "That's dumb. Writing is simple," she informed me. "Like Ms. Elbert always says, just say what you mean."

"It's not that easy," I said. "It's not like I'm writing a book report."

"It doesn't matter what you're writing," Addie answered patiently.

"Yeah? Well, maybe Ms. Elbert should come over and write the letter for me," I said.

"You're hilarious." Addie yawned and strolled out of the room.

I stared after her. Maybe she and Ms. Elbert were right. Maybe I was making this harder than I had to. Maybe it was simple. Why couldn't I just say what I wanted to say?

Dear Kristin,

I stared at the cursor.

Oh, forget it. I couldn't write this letter. No one could.

Frustrated, I switched off the computer. I was no good with written words ever. The only way I could tell her anything was in person. Or on the phone.

I picked up the phone and dialed before I lost my nerve. Before I thought about the fact that I wouldn't be anonymous if I spoke to her.

Her phone machine picked up on the second ring.

Hi, you've reached the Seltzers! We can't
take your call right now, but—

I slammed down the phone.

What was I thinking? The sound of her voice made me sick to my stomach. It was so familiar. I could imagine her smiling when she heard my voice leaving a message. But after she heard what I had to say, I could see her smile fade. See her look sick.

No. I couldn't give her the worst news of her entire life—on a machine.

"Hey, sports fan!" Billy appeared in the doorway, spinning a basketball with one hand, his favorite trick. "How about some one-on-one?"

"You're talking to me?" I asked. "I'm the enemy, remember?"

Billy looked hurt. "I never said that," he told me, tucking the ball under his arm. "Look, Brian, I just don't want you to make a mistake. Don't blow it for Mike—that's all I ever said. I'm just looking out for a friend. And I'm also looking out for you. People will remember this once you're at Sweet Valley High—and they might not like it. You get that, don't you?"

"Yeah, I guess." The trouble was, I did get it. Billy isn't mean, and he isn't stupid. He had a point. And I knew that he would change the whole situation if he could.

Billy tossed the basketball at my chest. I caught it and leaped up, aiming it at his head.

"Whoa!" Billy snatched the ball out of the air and whipped it behind his back, faking passes.

"Okay, let's go," I told him. A few minutes of basketball was probably just what I needed.

We hit the driveway and started shooting hoops. Billy blocked me about a dozen times. I sank a couple of good shots, though. Billy scored but fumbled the ball. I lunged at it, going for the rebound. But I got tangled up somehow and tripped myself. I crashed to the driveway.

I skinned my knee pretty badly, right through my jeans. It stung so much that tears filled my eyes. I turned away so Billy couldn't see. How

113

mortifying—I could feel my face turning red. *I will not cry*, I silently willed.

Billy leaned over me. "Ouch." He lightly punched my shoulder. "I took a fall like that last week," he said. "It even made me cry—can you believe it?"

I looked up at him. Billy was wearing shorts, and there was no scrape on either one of his knees. Besides, I hadn't seen him cry for years.

He was lying.

He was lying for me.

Suddenly I felt sure that Billy would never let me down. And I owed him the same thing—no matter what.

Billy reached out a hand, and I let him pull me up.

"Thanks," I said.

He grinned and stole the ball away. "Hey, that's what brothers are for."

He was right.

Elizabeth

Diary:

That's it, that's it, that's it! I've had it!

Jessica borrowed my favorite red sweater today without telling me she was going to and then spilled a milk shake on it!

And she won't even apologize!

I'm not speaking to her anymore.

Jessica

Friday, 3:20 P.M.

Dear Diary,

Elizabeth is out of control!

I borrowed her sweater today, and she flipped out just because I got a tiny little spot on the sleeve. I mean, is it really such a big deal? Has she forgotten about the time she totally spilled Gatorade all over my green velvet jacket at the Manchester Club?

I can't deal with her anymore.

I'm never going to talk to her again.

Brian

"Brian, toss me the chips!" Billy held out his hand. I lobbed the bag of chips his way. He reached out to catch it. But my dad leaped in front of him and grabbed the bag instead.

"Pass intercepted!" Dad opened the bag and grabbed a handful, then handed the bag to Billy. "Stay alert, Rainey," he teased.

"Right, Coach." Billy saluted Dad.

Mom stuck her head into the family room. "Don't fill up on snacks," she warned. "There's only an hour till dinner. And it's Friday, so you know what that means."

"Meat loaf," Billy said with a knowing look.

I wished I felt like eating. Meat loaf is one of my favorite things and a Friday-night ritual at our house. So is watching a game together when we can. If there's anything going on cable, my dad makes sure he gets off work a little early. He, Billy, Addie, and I camp out together in the family room. Mom, Ellie, and Sam aren't into

ball games, so they take care of cooking and set-
ting the table. Then all the sports addicts handle
cleanup. It's kind of fun usually.

But usually it's not the night of the Doggie
Chow dinner.

I glanced over at Dad and Billy. They were
both busy, stuffing their faces with chips and
sodas despite what Mom said. Addie was trying
to get better reception on the TV. Everything
seemed perfectly normal. One big, happy family,
just like always.

But I knew it wasn't true. Not the happy part
anyway. Not me.

Addie got back to the couch. She'd just
grabbed a soda when she stood up and shouted,
"Yes!"

Dad and Billy high-fived each other.

Billy thumped me on the back. "What a shot!"
he said. "Brian—was that incredible?"

"Uh, yeah," I said, even though I'd barely seen
it. "Amazing."

Billy thumped me on the back again, grinning
like crazy. "Our boys are all over it," he said.
"Lakers in the house!"

I gave him a lame smile and sneaked a glance
at the clock for the umpteenth time.

6:01.

Dad, Addie, and Billy thought it was an exciting,

fast-paced game. I felt like it was taking hours. Years.

I kept watching the clock, thinking, *Only one and a half hours left till Kristin's date. One hour and twenty minutes. One hour and seven minutes.*

By the time the game ended, my stomach was churning. No way could I handle meat loaf. I was practically sweating. I guess my family was so worked up about the game that they didn't notice anything was wrong with me.

"Dinner, everyone," Ellie called from the kitchen.

I followed Dad and Billy to the table. "Good game?" Mom asked. Addie gave her a play-by-play while I fiddled with my water glass and pretended to eat, pushing the food around my plate.

"Something wrong, Brian?" Mom asked me.

I started to answer, but Addie cut me off.

"Mom! Sam has more mashed potatoes than I do," Addie insisted.

"That's a total lie," Sam replied. "Besides, you got more meat loaf."

"Who cares?" Addie was pouting. "I don't even like meat loaf!"

"Stop it, girls," Mom said patiently. "There's enough for everyone to have seconds."

I was kind of glad Mom forgot about me. I didn't feel like explaining why I felt so horrible.

Billy wolfed down his food, then pushed back

his chair and got up, still wiping his mouth with his napkin. "That was great, Mom. May I be excused? I've got to go."

"Go where?" Dad asked.

"I've got a club meeting tonight. At seven-thirty," Billy added, checking his watch. "I've got to change."

"Wait a minute," I said, dropping my fork. "What club meeting?"

"You know." Billy shot me a warning look. "That big meeting we talked about."

I think my mouth dropped open in surprise. The Doggie Chow? Billy was going to the Doggie Chow? But—but he thought the whole thing was stupid! He couldn't be going. He'd never said he was!

"You're excused, Billy," Mom said. Billy smiled and carried his plate to the kitchen.

Kristin's going to see him there, I thought. She would see him there, and she would know that I knew. She would know that I could've helped her and I didn't.

Billy glanced at me on his way back from taking out his plate, then stalked out of the dining room and toward the stairs.

"Hang on," I said, following him into the hallway.

"Brian! You haven't been excused," Mom called. "And there's dessert."

"Sorry." I backtracked into the dining room. "May I please be excused?" I didn't give her enough time to say no. "Leave the dishes for me," I called over my shoulder as I took the stairs two at a time. "I'll clean up later. I promise!"

I found Billy already changing into his best clothes. A white button-down shirt, a tie, clean black jeans, and a blazer.

"You can't do this," I blurted out. "You never said anything about going to the dinner."

"What difference does it make?" Billy asked.

"A big difference," I shot back. "Having you there makes it worse. It's almost like I was there. How can you face Kristin, knowing you set her up?" How could I let him go there, knowing that I hadn't stopped the date?

Billy's face looked grim. "I don't have a choice about it any more than Mike does."

"Yes, you do, Billy," I said firmly. "You *both* have a choice."

He ignored me, pulling on his boots.

"And so do I," I added slowly. I hadn't really thought about it before, but it was true. All along I'd acted like I didn't have a choice. I didn't want to tell Kristin the truth because it would hurt her feelings too much. And I didn't want to go against my brother. But Kristin's feelings were about to be hurt big time, whether I told her the truth or not.

And sticking by my brother when he was acting like a jerk only made me a jerk too.

Billy's eyes narrowed. "Be careful, Brian. You could end up making a lot of enemies over this thing."

"Who cares?" I demanded. "Has it even occurred to you that this affects my life? Whether I tell Kristin the truth or not, this situation affects me." I stared at him. Why was it my job to be the loyal brother? Couldn't Billy see that he was being disloyal to me by even allowing this to happen?

Billy looked like he couldn't believe what he was hearing. "What are you saying?" he asked. "Are you saying you're going to side with Kristin over me? Your own brother?"

"I'm sorry, Billy." I know my voice sounded sad because I was sad. Sad that Billy couldn't be the one to make all of this all right. He was older—he was supposed to know what to do. But it isn't always that easy, I guess. Otherwise I would have done the right thing a lot sooner. "You may be my brother, but this is wrong. You're wrong. I won't go along with this." We stared at each other, and in that moment I made up my mind. "I'm going to warn Kristin," I said.

Billy grabbed my arm. "Calm down," he said. "Do you want to ruin this whole night?"

"Yes," I told him, wrenching my arm out of

Billy's grip and pulling away. "Kristin is my friend. Too good a friend to lose over some stupid prank."

Billy didn't say anything as I clambered down the stairs. The front door slammed behind me. I think my mom yelled something, but I didn't stop to listen. It was already past seven. The dinner started at seven-thirty.

I ran the whole way to Kristin's block. I could hardly breathe by the time I got to her corner, but I felt good. It was the kind of feeling you get only when you know you're right. Then I looked across the street at her house.

I stopped dead in my tracks. My whole body went cold.

Mike's car was parked at the curb, but there was no sign of Mike. He was already inside.

I was too late.

Elizabeth

Dear Diary,
So Jessica is giving me the silent treatment. She didn't say word one all through dinner.
Big deal.

Jessica

Friday, 7:23 P.M.

Dear Diary,
If Elizabeth thinks that I'm going to speak to her first, she's going to have a long time to think about it.

Elizabeth

Dear Diary,

I am so mad at Jessica that I can't even concentrate on my homework!

Jessica

Dear Diary,
I'm bored.

Friday, 8:43 P.M.

Elizabeth

Dear Diary,

It wouldn't really be talking to Jessica if I asked for my sweater back, would it?

I mean, it's mine.

Jessica

Friday, 9:14 P.M.

Dear Diary,
    I don't want Elizabeth's gross sweater in here anymore.
    I'm going to give it back to her.
    But I won't apologize.

Kristin

"You look beautiful. Just beautiful!"
Mom was about to give me a hug, but she
stopped herself. "I don't want to mess up your
hair," she said.

I laughed, catching her eye in the mirror.

I looked great. The dress looked great.
Everything looked great. My hair was perfect—in
an updo with these curly tendrils hanging down.

Mom helped me with my makeup. She knew
a few tricks from when she was a model. I had to
admit, she had a gift. Everything was done with a
light touch—not too much liner, no clumpy
mascara. I looked like myself, only tons better.

"Lacey was certainly right about this dress,"
Mom said, eyeing me with approval. "It really
makes the most of your figure."

I couldn't believe it! For once she wasn't
going to give me a lecture about losing weight.
The fact was, this dress couldn't have looked any
better no matter how thin I was.

"I never would have picked red for your skin tone," Mom went on. "But that shade is perfect. It just lights you up." She was so excited, she actually clapped.

Mom gets carried away sometimes, but I didn't mind it tonight.

I had a feeling that nothing could ruin this evening.

"Hold it, I'm going to take a picture." Mom ran to the closet to dig out her camera. I checked my pearl earrings to make sure they weren't going to fall out.

The doorbell rang.

Mike!

I thought my stomach would drop down to my toes. I swallowed hard and took an extra-deep breath. I checked out the small window by the front door. I could see Mike outside. He was wearing a dark gray suit with a blue shirt and yellow tie. He looked awesome, but he was shifting his weight from foot to foot, as if he was nervous. I smiled. At least I knew I wasn't the only one.

"I'll get it," I called.

I opened the door. Mike started to say hello, but the words died on his lips.

He stared. I mean, we are talking bug-eyed. In the best way possible.

Suddenly I was almost glad for all those times

that Mike had seen me looking like a slob. He obviously couldn't believe how good I looked.

"Wow," he said. He just stood there with that bug-eyed look on his face.

"Come in," I told him. I did this cool, slow-blink thing that Lacey had taught me.

"What?" he asked, blinking a couple of times.

"Come in," I repeated. It was a real effort not to giggle.

"Oh. Oh—right." He entered the hall just as Mom appeared with her camera.

"This is Mike," I said quickly. "And we're running kind of late. . . ." I didn't want Mom to hang around too long and give him the third degree.

She gave him a big smile and stuck out her hand. "It's so nice to meet you, Mike," she said. "Do you mind if I take one picture?" she asked as they shook hands.

I groaned. "Mo-o-om," I said through clenched teeth.

"It's okay," Mike said. "No problem." He put his arm around me for the picture, and I noticed that his palm was kind of sweaty. Normally that would have grossed me out, but I thought it was too cute that this gorgeous guy was actually nervous about going on a date with me.

The flashbulb went off, and Mom tucked the camera away. "You two have a nice time," she said. Another miracle! No long conversation about school, and no Inquisition-style questions about Mike's plans for the future. Although she did add, "Don't stay out too late. And drive carefully, Mike. You're carrying precious cargo!"

I groaned again.

Mike cleared his throat. "Uh, sure, I will, Mrs. Seltzer. We should hurry, I guess," he added, turning to me. He looked like he didn't know if he should take my arm or not. We sort of stood there for a minute, but in the end Mike didn't take my arm. Instead he opened the front door for me.

That's when I saw him.

Brian?

He was standing in the middle of my front walk. Just standing there. *What is he doing here?*

I think I said his name out loud. I'm not sure. We just stared at each other for a moment.

"Wow," Brian said, looking at my dress.

"What are you doing here?" I blurted out. "No, don't say anything," I added.

I turned to Mike. He was looking at Brian uncertainly. "Hey, Brian," he said, but it came out sounding like a question. I had no idea what either one of them was thinking.

"Brian's always dropping by," I told Mike quickly. I forced myself to smile as if nothing was wrong.

"Sorry, Bri, I'm busy tonight," I sang out, trying to pull Mike past him.

But Brian wouldn't let us pass—he stepped directly in front of us and shot Mike the nastiest look I've ever seen Brian give anyone. The nastiest look I've ever seen, period.

"Brian, what's going on?" I demanded.

Brian turned to me. "I, uh, this is a—a big mistake," he stammered.

"What?" I couldn't believe my ears. "Brian, get out of the way."

"No." Brian flushed a dark red. He looked at Mike. "You know, you're a real jerk."

Mike made a weird choking noise.

"Brian!" I glared at him. "Are you crazy? What is wrong with you?"

"Kristin, believe me, you don't want to go on this date," Brian said.

"Don't tell me what I want to do, Brian!" I shouted. "You don't know me as well as you think you do. And I obviously don't know you either! I can't believe you would do this to me—I will never, ever forgive you." Tears stung my eyes, and I blinked them away.

"Kristin—," Brian said, "please. Please don't cry—"

"Let's go," I said, grabbing Mike's arm and practically yanking him past Brian.

I didn't look back. I got into the car and stared straight ahead, trying not to cry. I didn't even glance at Mike. I couldn't.

Mike didn't say anything either. I think he was too shocked to speak. He started the motor and pulled away from the curb.

I couldn't believe this. I'd dreamed about this moment every day this week. And now it was ruined! I took a couple of deep breaths. *If I cry, then my mascara will run, and I'll look terrible,* I thought, willing myself to calm down. *Okay, just because Brian is a freak doesn't mean that this whole date with Mike has to be awful. I can get past this.*

I felt a little better by the time we pulled into the driveway of Jordan Kander's house. Jordan is the captain of the wrestling team at SVH—he's totally cool.

I managed to keep a pleasant expression on my face as we walked into Jordan's family room, even though I still felt a little shaky. Mike hadn't said a word since we left my house. I wondered what his take on that whole scene with Brian was. It must have looked utterly bizarre to him. After all, even I wasn't sure what it was about.

Well, it's time to set the damage control in motion, I thought as I checked out the room. A long table was set out, filling the space. The table looked nice, covered with a pretty paper tablecloth and matching plates, napkins, and cups.

"Um, this is nice," I told Mike.

"Yeah," he answered. He was staring at his shoes, though.

"So where are Jordan's parents?" I asked.

Mike glanced up at me in surprise. "They're out of town. That's why we're having the party here."

"Oh," I squeaked. How could I be such a dork? These were high school guys—of course they had parties without adults around. *Mike must think I'm a total idiot,* I thought. *And he must think my friends are idiots, too.*

I wished desperately that I could think of something to say that would ease the tension, but I couldn't think of anything besides, "Aren't my friends insane?" or "That Brian—I wish he would just say no to drugs. Ha, ha!"

I decided I'd better stay away from the subject.

Thankfully, one of Mike's friends came over then and clapped him on the back. "Hey, Mike-o," he said. Then he turned to me. "I'm Walker."

"Nice to meet you," I told him.

"And this is Suzanne," Walker went on, gesturing toward his date.

"Hi," she said, and I smiled.

"I love your dress." I stepped back to admire the deep blue-green color. It was kind of shimmery.

"Thanks," she replied, pushing up her glasses. That's when I noticed that her eyes were the same color as her dress—though her lenses were so thick that you had to look at her closely to notice. *She has such pretty eyes,* I thought. *What a shame—I guess her prescription is too strong for contacts.*

I scanned the crowd, wondering whether any of Lacey's friends were there. But I didn't see Annie or Sara or anyone else who looked familiar. Oh, well. *I just need to mingle,* I decided.

I headed for the punch bowl. While I was pouring myself a drink, I felt someone come up behind me.

"Would you like a glass of punch?" I asked without turning around to see who it was.

The person didn't respond. "Would you like some punch?" I repeated, turning around this time.

"I'm sorry," said a pretty, dark-haired girl behind me. "Were you speaking to me?"

"Punch?" I held up my glass.

"Sure, thanks," she said. "I'm Carla."

"Kristin." I handed her the glass and poured myself another. Then I turned back to Carla, and we started talking about what a nice house Jordan had. Carla's hair was cut very short—a really cute style, one that would look horrendous on me. As I was admiring it, I noticed that she had hearing aids in both ears. *No wonder she couldn't hear me when I asked about the punch!* I realized with a jolt. I made a mental note to remember to speak slowly and enunciate when I spoke to Carla.

"So, who's your date?" I asked her.

"Terry," she said, pointing to a tall, blond guy across the room.

"He's cute," I said, and grinned at her.

"I've had a crush on Terry forever," Carla admitted, looking at the ceiling in this I-can't-believe-this-is-happening-to-me kind of way. "I never even thought he knew I existed."

"That is so cool," I told her. *Wow,* I thought. *These wrestling-team guys are really awesome.* Not that wearing a hearing aid is a big deal, but I knew that some of the guys at SVJH might make a big deal out of it. In fact, as I scanned the room again, I realized that most of the wrestling-team members' dates weren't beautiful in the traditional way. Don't get me wrong—everyone looked great, and all of the girls had on terrific outfits. It's just that when you live in California, you get used to a sort of sun-streaked-blond-hair, size-six-figure type of beauty. But these girls were individuals—they all looked different.

I guess this is what it's like when you grow up, I realized happily. *Guys know how to spot more than one kind of beauty.* I couldn't wait to go home and tell my mom that I was never going on another diet again.

Looking around the room again, I spotted Billy Rainey. He was sitting in a corner, goofing around with some of the guys.

Billy was here? Well, I guessed that made sense. He was on the wrestling team too. It just seemed weird. Brian knew I was coming to this party, but he never said anything about Billy being here. Then again, Brian had been acting less than normal lately.

I caught Billy's eye and waved. He looked away quickly without waving back.

I frowned. What was that all about? I wondered whether Billy knew about Brian's big freak-out tonight. Maybe he was just embarrassed because of his brother.

Mike walked up to me. "Hungry?" he asked.

I shrugged. "Not really," I answered. It was true. There were too many excited butterflies floating around in my stomach for me to even think about food.

Mike and I stood there awkwardly for a moment. "I think they're getting ready to serve dinner," Mike said. "Should we go sit down?"

"Let's," I said. Other people were starting to move toward the tables. Mike and I took a seat across from Carla and her date.

Mike and I sat in silence for a moment. *Say something,* I told myself.

"This is a pretty big room," I said finally, desperate to get Mike talking. "Do you know all the guys here? I've never met any of the girls before." Mike just nodded, staring at his plate. Not a word. My heart sank. This date was turning into a total disaster. I'd never forgive Brian! Obviously Mike was still upset. I felt my throat tighten.

"Well, actually, I sort of know some of the girls," I went on in a rush. As if talking more would make this date all right. "At least I do now, you know, because I've been talking to a couple of—"

"Look, Kristin," Mike suddenly blurted out, turning to me. "I—"

I stopped talking. I leaned forward, eager to hear whatever he might say. Anything!

"I, uh . . ." He stopped and stared at his plate again. "I want you to know that, well, that I—"

A burst of cheers and clapping cut him off. Four guys appeared, carrying big platters of food. "Dinner is served," one of them announced.

"I just want you to know that I'm sorry," Mike finished.

"Oh—you mean about Brian?" I asked. "Me too." A wave of relief washed over me—at least the ice was broken. Now I could eat in peace.

Two of the guys made their way down each side of our table, dishing food onto the girls' plates. I stared down at mine.

For a minute I wondered whether Jordan had tried to cook the food himself. Poor guy—it hadn't come out too well. My pretty, flowered plate was covered with lumpy, brown glop. A thick sauce oozed out of it. Some of the sauce dripped over the edge of the plate. It landed in a soggy puddle on the tablecloth.

And it smelled weird. Kind of familiar.

I stifled a giggle. If I didn't know any better, I'd think this was dog food.

I glanced at Mike to see if he thought Jordan's attempt at cooking was as funny as I did. He was staring at me. His face was entirely red, and his mouth was hanging open. I felt the smile drop off my face.

What was going on? Mike's expression—I could only call it horror.

"Woof! Arf! Arf!"

One of the serving guys started to bark. A few others joined in. Soon the whole room erupted into wild barking sounds. I stared across the table at Carla. Her eyebrows were drawn together in confusion. She obviously didn't know what was going on any more than I did.

I turned back to Mike, who had started laughing.

But the laughter sounded nervous, and his face was still scarlet. The guys around me kept on barking. I looked back down at my plate. . . . For some reason, Brian popped into my mind. I thought about what he had said to Mike, "You know, you're a real jerk." And to me, "Kristin, believe me, you don't want to go on this date. . . ."

His words echoed in my mind. Suddenly it all made sense. Dog food. Barking . . . what are these guys saying? That they think their dates are dogs?

I sat back, stunned.

Mike thinks—he thinks I'm a dog?

I was having trouble breathing. I couldn't get enough air—my throat was too tight.

My face started to burn.

I should have known, I should have known, I should have known. . . . My brain repeated it endlessly. *I should have known that a guy like Mike would never want to go out with me.* . . . All week I'd felt so beautiful. So special. I should have known it was all a lie.

My mother had been right all along.

The smell of the dog food hit my nostrils, and for a moment I thought I might vomit.

How could I have been so stupid? I stared down at my hands. My palms felt hot, as if my whole body was burning with shame.

Someone made a weird, strangling sound. A sob. For a second, I swear, I thought it was me.

But when I looked up, I realized that it was Carla.

She was just sitting there, perfectly still, crying. She was looking down at the table while tears streamed down her face. "I've had a crush on Terry forever," she'd told me. "I never even thought he knew I existed. . . ." I looked across the table at Terry—I watched him laughing. *Laughing* at this perfectly sweet girl, as if he were better than she was. As if he were some great prize and she was just a little nobody.

My whole body started burning even worse than before. Burning with rage.

Slowly I pushed back my chair.

The laughing went on and on as I stood up. I glanced down at Mike. He actually looked afraid as I raised my fist in the air.

I brought it down with all the force I possessed and slammed it on the table. Mike cringed and jumped back. I guess he thought I was going to hit him.

The table shook, and the laughter fell silent.

"Really funny!" I shouted. I looked down the table and stared Terry in the eye. "Big joke," I went on, more quietly this time. Terry shifted in his chair and looked away.

"You guys think you're so smooth, don't you?"

I demanded. "You're so cool that this is your idea of fun?" I looked around the table. "Billy? Are you having a good time now?"

He didn't respond. He didn't even look at me.

I tried to keep my voice from trembling with anger. "Do you really think looks are all that matter? Is that the way you judge another person?" I paused. "Well, that isn't what I've learned. What really makes someone a winner is the way they treat other people. Which means you guys are the biggest bunch of losers I've ever met. You'd be lucky to have girls like us—but you don't deserve us. None of you."

I reached across the table and lifted Carla's chin. She was still crying as I looked her in the eye. "Carla," I said slowly and distinctly, "we're leaving."

She sniffled, then nodded. She stood up. One or two of the other girls stood up too. My heart soared. *We're out of here,* I thought.

Carla grabbed her purse, then stopped when her eye fell on the plate of dog food.

For a minute I was afraid that she would break down again. *Don't cry, Carla,* I silently willed her. *Let's just go.*

But Carla reached down and picked up the plate of dog food. Then she dumped it in Terry's lap.

"Gross!" he shouted, leaping up and wiping his lap with a napkin.

"Ha!" Someone let out a loud laugh. I looked over. It was Suzanne. She started laughing, and she couldn't stop. She had to take off her glasses and wipe her eyes. Suzanne's whole body was shaking, and her shimmery blue dress was rustling.

All the girls stared at one another. Then Suzanne looked over at me, and I giggled too. I couldn't help it. I felt like I was releasing the tension of a whole week, and it felt good. Soon all the other girls were laughing too.

"See you later, losers!" I yelled.

Carla gave me a shaky smile. I jerked my head toward the door. The other girls grabbed their things and headed for the exit.

As I turned to go, Mike grabbed my wrist. "Kristin," he said. "I'm really sorry."

I nodded slowly. "Yes," I told him, "you really *are* sorry."

I jerked my wrist away and headed for the door. For a minute the doorway was so crammed with righteously angry females that I didn't even see him.

Brian stumbled to the side. "Kristin!" he called, waving frantically.

I blinked in surprise. Brian?

I felt a wide smile spread across my face. *He came to rescue me,* I realized. Then I giggled. *Too late!*

I crossed the room quickly. "I'm so glad you're here," I told him.

Brian let out a relieved sigh. "Me too," he said. Then he offered me his elbow. I put my arm through his, and we walked out of the dinner party, our heads held high.

Brian and I stepped out the front door and were suddenly looking down at a group of girls standing at the bottom of the stairs leading up to the house. Now that we were out of the house, a few more of them were crying. I guess they hadn't wanted their dates to see them upset. Carla was hugging a girl with short, brown hair, stroking her back and whispering to her. Suzanne was sitting in the grass, slumped over, as if she was too tired to stand.

One or two others were standing there, staring blankly into space. Trying to figure out what had happened to their magical night, I guess.

I knew the feeling.

Suddenly I felt like all of the air had been sucked from my body. A tear trickled down my nose. I looked down at my dress. Why had I even bought it? I should have known that no dress could ever make me beautiful when I wasn't. . . .

I started to sob and couldn't stop. All I could think about was how unfair it was. . . . This was

supposed to be the best night of my life. . . . I
couldn't help how I looked. . . .

Brian grabbed my hand and squeezed.

"Kristin!" I heard someone say.

I looked up and saw Carla striding toward
me. She put her arms around me and gave me a
hug. She patted my back as I kept crying.

"Thank you," she said quietly.

For what? I wanted to ask, but I didn't have a
chance. The girl with the short, brown hair had
already walked over and wrapped her arms
around us. "Thanks, Kristin," she said.

I looked over Carla's shoulder at Suzanne. She
nodded, then stood up and walked over to us.
"What would we have done without you?" Suzanne
asked.

"We would have eaten dog food!" the brown-
haired girl cried, and everyone else laughed.

Soon all of the girls had joined our group hug.

And Brian was still holding my hand, squeezing like he'd never let go.

I don't know how long we all stood there, but
it seemed like a long time. I began to feel less
horrible. *These girls aren't ugly,* I thought. *And I'm
one of them. Who cares what those guys think?*

"So," Suzanne said finally, "what do we do now?"

I sniffled a bit. Brian reached into his pocket
for a tissue.

"I don't know," I admitted. I blew my nose, which made everyone—including me—laugh. "I don't really feel like going home."

"Me either," the brown-haired girl agreed. The other girls nodded.

"Let's go dancing," Carla said suddenly.

I stared at her. "Dancing?" I asked.

"It'll be a victory dance." Carla grinned.

"Carla," I said slowly, "that is the best idea I have ever heard."

We extricated ourselves from our hug. Everyone chattered and giggled as we headed down the walk. At the end of the block we turned left, toward the Manchester Club. It's all teens there, and they play live music. Plus there was no doubt that half of SVJH would be there to see us doing our victory dance.

Brian and I hung back from the rest of the group. We walked along in silence for a while. I guess we were both thinking. He was still holding my hand.

Suddenly I let out a laugh. "So—what exactly were you going to do?" I asked him.

He looked confused.

"At the party, I mean," I went on. "When you busted in there at the end?"

He shrugged. "I have no idea," he admitted. "Punch Mike in the nose, maybe? Or Billy?"

"As if," I said, laughing at the thought of it. I squeezed his hand. "You're a good friend, Brian," I told him quietly.

Brian stopped walking and dropped my hand. "How can you even say that?" he demanded, his voice cracking. "I totally let you down. I should have told you about this from the start." He shook his head, and for a minute I thought I saw tears in his eyes. "I never should have let it get this far."

"Oh, Brian," I told him. "You tried to warn me. Besides, what could you have told me that wouldn't have hurt my feelings just as much as going to the party did? This really wasn't your fault," I said, peering up into his face. But he still looked so miserable that finally I stepped forward and gave him a hug. "Thanks for trying to save me," I whispered into his chest.

I let go and took a step back. I smiled at him. "And at least I got a new dress out of this whole thing," I said, putting one hand on my hip and striking a pose.

Brian grinned. "Some dress," he said, waggling his eyebrows.

We both laughed.

Then he turned more serious. "You really are beautiful, you know, Kristin," he said. Just like that. Like it was a fact that nobody could argue with. Brian looked at his shoes. "I've always thought so."

My eyes started to tear up again, but not from sadness this time. I just felt totally overwhelmed all of a sudden.

"Just in case you were confused," Brian added.

I smiled weakly. "Okay, Brian," I told him. I took a couple of deep breaths, then looked into his eyes. "Thanks."

Brian gave me an elaborate bow and offered me his arm again. I took it. The moon was bright and the air was crisp as we walked along. It was one of those nights right before the weather turns cold when everything seems clean and fresher than usual.

It felt like the beginning of something, somehow.

I took a deep breath, pulling the air deep into my lungs and smiled as Brian and I strolled down the street toward the Manchester Club, arm in arm.

Together.

Elizabeth

Dear Diary,

Jessica and I made up. We actually ended up in the bathroom at the same time last night—I was going to get my sweater, and she was coming to give it back. So, she apologized. Then I did too for grouching at her like I did. After all, there was the whole Gatorade/velvet jacket debacle to consider. These things happen.

Then Jessica asked me if I wanted her to do my nails. So we did that for a while. Then she said she needed some help with her English paper, so we worked on that until it was time to go to bed.

Not exactly a thrilling Friday night, but it could have been worse.

Only one more week of being grounded to go.

I wonder if we'll make it.

The *ONLY* Official Book on Today's Hottest Band!

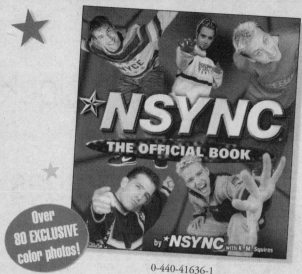

Over 80 EXCLUSIVE color photos!

0-440-41636-1

Get up close and personal with Justin, J.C., Lance, Chris, and Joey as they discuss—in their own words—their music, their friendships on and offstage, their fans, and much more!

On sale now wherever books are sold.

And don't miss

Available wherever music and videos are sold.